HELEN HUMPHREYS is an award-winning Canadian novelist and poet. She was born in London, England, and now lives in Kingston, Ontario. Humphreys' first novel, *Leaving Earth*, was a *New York Times* Notable Book in 1998 and won the City of Toronto Book Award. In 2009, Humphreys was awarded the Harbourfront Festival Prize for literary excellence. Her novel, *The Reinvention of Love*, and her memoir of her brother, *True Story*, are also published by Serpent's Tail.

Praise for *The Evening Chorus*

"A poised, lyrical novel about the griefs of war, written with poetic intensity of observation" Helen Dunmore

"*The Evening Chorus* serenades people brutally marked by war yet enduring to live the tiny pleasures of another day. With her trademark prose Humphreys convinces us of the birdlike strength of the powerless" Emma Donoghue

"Poignantly explores the sorrows of war and consolations of nature ... A story of heartbreak and hope, it unfolds against a mesmerizingly described natural world" *Mail on Sunday*

"In *The Evening Chorus* the interventions of war, and the resulting human tragedies, play out against a natural world at once remote, alien and ultimately redemptive. The novel has a crystalline quality about it—it's clear and complex and self-contained. It sparkles" Jo Baker, author of *Longbourn*

"Humphreys has spun an atmospheric yarn, and her descriptions of flora and fauna always engage" Stephanie Cross, *Daily Mail*

D0280505

THE
EVENING
CHORUS

THE
EVENING CHORUS

HELEN HUMPHREYS

A complete catalogue record for this book can
be obtained from the British Library on request

First published in 2015 by HarperCollins Publishers, Ltd, Toronto

First published in this edition in 2016

First published in the UK in 2015 by Serpent's Tail,
an imprint of Profile Books Ltd
3 Holford Yard
Bevin Way
London WC1X 9HD
www.serpentstail.com

ISBN 978 1 78125 303 8
eISBN 978 1 78283 087 0

Printed and bound by
CPI Group (UK) Ltd, Croydon CR0 4YY

1 3 5 7 9 10 8 6 4 2

Mixed Sources
Product group from well-managed
forests and other controlled sources
www.fsc.org Cert no. TT-COC-002227
© 1996 Forest Stewardship Council
FSC

For Phyllis Bruce

The dark swallows will return and again hang their nests on your balcony and strike your window with their wings. But those that slowed their flight to see your beauty, and those that learnt your name and mine, those won't return.

—Gustavo Adolfo Bécquer

1940

Redstart

James Hunter falls through morning.

He swings from his parachute harness as the plane drops below him, the broken shell of the bomber sinking into the Channel fog.

The water is as jarring as solid earth, and shockingly cold.

"Here! I'm over here!" yells Roberts, the pilot of the Wellington.

James fumbles to unclip himself from the parachute, then swims towards the pilot's voice and the shadow of the rubber dinghy bobbing in the swell. His bomber jacket and life vest allow only a stuttering breaststroke, and when he flips over on his back to rest for a moment, James notices that the vest has been ripped open above his heart. In the scramble from the cockpit, the canvas must have caught on a piece of sheared fuselage and torn.

He touches the edges of the incision gingerly, as though it were his own flesh that had been sliced open, and the white fluff inside the life preserver lifts into the air, a few strands of the kapok floss drifting slowly upwards, small brown seeds swinging from the fibres.

The shushing of the waves is suddenly interrupted by the whine of an engine.

James Hunter takes a deep breath, blows it out under the floss, and watches as the tiny parachutes rise up into the fog and disappear.

There's a moment when he's hopeful that it's a British ship, but after James blinks in the bright glare of the searchlight, he sees the shine of a black boot resting on the gunwale and above that a gloved hand holding a pistol.

"*Hier!*" yells the soldier at the bow of the boat to the soldiers in the stern. "*Es gibt einen hier!*"

The engine cuts out immediately, and the soldier with the pistol leans over the gunwale. He grins at his captive, floating in the early morning chop, and says, clearly and in English:

"For you, the war is over."

THE COMMUNAL shower in the delousing building reminds James of boarding school. He places his kit neatly in the cardboard box with his name on it, then walks into the showers cupping his genitals with the same protective modesty he displayed when he was twelve and forced to take swimming lessons in the brackish pond behind the school library. The hot blast of water is a relief after the cold of the sea. His newly and hastily shaven head stings when the shower water hits it.

What started out as his six-man bomber crew has multiplied at the delousing facility into a hundred or so men, all of whom share the indignity of being captured within the same twenty-four-hour period.

Under the statutes of the Geneva Conventions, prisoners of war are allowed to wear their own uniforms. When the box with James's clothes is returned to him, his uniform is warm and smells like almonds.

"Cyanide," says the soldier next to him when he sees James sniffing his jacket like a dog. "They think it kills the lice and stops the typhus."

"The Jerries are more afraid of the louse than they are of us," mutters a man farther down the bench.

But the louse will torment all of them in the prison camp. It will be worse than the boredom, the filth, and the food. The small insect, only the size of a sesame seed, will live in the clothing of the men, crawling onto their bodies to feed and then returning to the clothing to rest. In James's bunkhouse, the frantic slapping and jerky movements of a prisoner trying to kill the lice while they're sucking his blood become known as "dancing the jig."

Once, James wakes up to the sounds of a man crying and sees Stevens sitting at the table in the centre of the room. He's naked, his back covered in red sores from louse bites.

"I can't do it," he says when James climbs down from his bunk. "I can't put it back on."

Stevens's uniform lies crumpled on the floor. It is so cold in the barracks that James can see his breath. He lights the candle inside the tin can on the table and picks up his bunkmate's jacket. With the same precision that would have been used to sew that jacket, he holds each seam over the flame, moving along the stitch just before the fabric catches fire. The swollen bodies of the lice make a small pop as they burst their cargo of blood above the candle.

THE OFLAG, set deep inside the newly drawn borders of Bavaria, was a barracks for Polish prisoners during the first war, and the large limestone buildings, already on the grounds, have been taken by the Germans for their quarters.

James can see the German quarters from the window that borders his top bunk. At first he monitors the activity around the buildings, watching the guards come and go, paying attention when the Kommandant steps out onto the wooden platform that has been constructed along the front of his office. But when it becomes clear that the war is going to continue for some time, and that James isn't getting out of the prison camp, he loses interest in observing the Germans and begins to monitor the buildings themselves.

When it rains, the limestone turns a darker grey. In a heavy rain, the outside of the buildings stays wet for ages and gives off the flat smell of clay, noticeable when the men are gathered on parade at the beginning and end of every day. James wonders if the damp of the stone extends all the way into the interior of the structure—if the stone is so porous as to conduct moisture through walls that appear to be over a foot thick.

The geologist in bunkhouse 2 has told him that limestone is formed from prehistoric marine life, from all the shells and dead sea creatures that collect at the bottom of the ocean and are compressed, over millions of years, into sedimentary rock. When James watches the barrack walls darken in the rain, he is reminded of the deep shade of the ocean, how it slopes off under the hull of a fishing boat. The darkness of the ocean always seemed empty to him, but now he thinks of the rock slowly forming along the seabed—a rock made of creatures that live in water. A rock essentially made from water.

With the exception of the squadron leader, whose rank still means something in the camp, most of the men have reverted to the identity they had before the war. The geologist was a lecturer at Oxford. The writer worked in an advertising agency. The actor was fairly well known in the West End. James was a grammar school science teacher. But gradually, with the days and weeks that accumulate, these prisoners of war start to become known for their roles within the camp. The geologist becomes the Gardener. The writer, good at cards and winning a large portion of the other men's monthly cigarette ration, becomes the Gambler. The actor, however, stays the Actor, setting up camp theatricals; he is busier than he was in civilian life, not only performing in the productions but directing and writing them as well, and helping to sew the costumes.

James, shot down on his first mission as an RAF pilot in training, doesn't mind losing a rank he hadn't even earned yet. For a while he is called the Teacher, but he soon loses this title to the label that best describes his activity in the camp—the Birdman.

THE PRISONERS are housed in eighteen hastily constructed one-storey wooden bunkhouses, each holding fourteen rooms with eight men per room. Each of these rooms has a coal-burning stove, a table, and four bunk beds, one on each wall. Right now James has a desk because he has constructed one using a few of the slats that hold his mattress, but during these cold winter months, all available wood will be consigned to the stove, and James knows his desk will be the first thing to go. In the bunkhouse room beside his, the chair and table legs have already been burned and the remaining furniture jokingly suspended from the ceiling with string taken from around the Red Cross parcels.

The bunkhouses are made of pine, a soft wood that burns quickly, the rougher planks sometimes hissing with resin inside the stove, a sound very much like summer rain falling on hot, dry ground. The soft wood is easy to manipulate when floor-boards need to be pried up for tunnels or mattress slats snapped for kindling. Because the wood is so roughly milled, the pine boards on the walls of the bunkhouse have a multitude of knots, and the pris-oners work these out and use the space behind them to store small items that they don't want the guards or their fellow bunkmates to find—wedding rings, letters, the German-issued identity tags, which the prisoners don't wear but feel they can't lose or destroy. Some of the prisoners use their new identity tags as tools to cut bread and slice the canned meat rolls that arrive in the Red Cross parcels.

When James is bashing the circuit in the evening with Stevens and the Gardener, he doesn't look down at his feet as they walk around and around the perimeter of the camp. Instead he looks out, beyond the wire, to the sky and the forest. The pine trees grow closely together, barely any space between them. When a prisoner escapes he invariably heads into this dense forest, hoping to reach the other side, where there is a small town with a train station. If the escape has been a long time in the planning, the prisoner will have made a false identity with the help of the Artist, and he will hope to board the train as a passenger. If the escape is a sudden one, brought on by opportunity rather than plotting, then the prisoner will attempt to stow away on a freight train. After an escape, James can hear the barking of the Alsatian dogs as they are sent into the forest to find the prisoner; almost always, he is discovered crouching among the leaves or running towards town, and is back in camp within twenty-four hours.

At the edge of the forest is a fir tree surrounded by four birch trees, the white of the bark standing out among the green pines. The birches, encircling the fir, look like they have caught it, enclosing it in a sort of cage.

"It's just like us," said Stevens, when James first pointed it out to him.

Stevens circuit-bashes with James in the evenings, but otherwise he remains in his bunk, reading novels. In the air force he was a pilot. In civilian life he was a law student. In camp he is known as the Reader.

At first James looked at the fir tree trapped by the birches as Stevens did, but gradually he has come to see it differently. The fir has been forced to grow straight up as it looks for a way out of the trees that hold it captive. As a result, it is taller than the other pines, able to claim a larger quotient of sunlight. Also, the cage around it keeps it from being toppled by wind. And what if trees that grow so closely together have a relationship that is invisible to the human observer? What if they communicate through their root systems, through the exhalations from their leaves? James remembers his grandfather, who was a fisherman, telling him that the tallest, straightest pines were chosen as masts for the old brigs and barques because pine, even when dead, still has flexibility in it, will still move a little with the weight of wind in sails, and yet will also stand firm.

"The wind in the pines sounds exactly like the sea, like waves on the shingle," said a man who had escaped and been recaptured after spending the night lost in the forest.

As James moves around the camp at dusk, he also moves from thinking of the pine tree as a captive to thinking of it as the centre of a family, and in this way he recognizes that he himself has started to change, that he has begun to think of the prison camp not as home, but certainly as the place where he now lives.

ON THREE sides of the camp is a wire fence with wooden guard towers at each corner. The fence is twelve feet high and made of double-thick barbed wire. Fifteen inches inside the fence is a tripwire set a foot off the ground. Any prisoner who steps over this wire, even to retrieve a football, is shot.

Everything possible has been done by the Germans to deter prisoners from escaping. The bunkhouses are raised on wooden pilings, to discourage tunnelling. The guards in the towers are armed with machine guns and searchlights that sweep the compound in random patterns, so there is no predicting where the safe pockets of darkness will fall if someone dares to make a run for it. At night the guards are doubled and unleash their Alsatian dogs, which race around the compound, sniffing out any hidden escapees.

Prisoners are locked inside the bunkhouses until morning roll call, which happens at sunrise, when all two thousand men are roused from their bunks to stand in the muddy yard that separates the bunkhouses from the more spacious quarters of the Germans. The men stand in a long line facing the Kommandant, who remains on the verandah of his office during the procedure, strutting up and down, his chest puffed out like a winter robin's. In the evening after supper, there is another roll call.

By the laws of the Geneva Conventions, officers who are prisoners are not required to work, and this endless stretch of leisure time is hard on those who do not have a pursuit or passion to occupy them. For the men who seek activity, sport and gardening are favourites.

But escape is the most popular pastime.

From the moment he arrived at the Oflag, James was given the information he needed to escape, the arithmetic of the camp.

It is three hundred feet from the corner of the closest bunkhouse to the wire, and another thirty feet outside the wire to the ditch. The ditch is ten feet across. Beyond the ditch is the forest, beyond the forest the road, beyond the road the town. If a man were able to dig a foot an hour, undetected, during the available daylight hours between roll calls, it would still take three months to get outside the wire.

James has no desire to escape. He doesn't think it's an accident that the nearest bunkhouse to the wire is still three hundred feet from it. The Germans have also done the arithmetic, and they have calculated that three months is just long enough for them to discover any tunnel under construction.

It occurs to James that perhaps the Germans want the prisoners to attempt escape, that this little game of cat and mouse keeps both sides interested and occupied during the months of mind-numbing boredom in the prison camp.

Prisoners who tunnel are called "moles" because they work like those animals, digging with their hands to fashion a tunnel barely wider than their own bodies, using their hands as flippers to push the freshly dug earth behind them, where it is gathered up by other prisoners. What to do with the soil remains the biggest problem in escape attempts, as the newly dug earth is not the same colour or texture as the pale sand that covers the surface of the camp. It cannot simply be blended in. A certain amount can be distributed in the gardens, but the rest has to be hidden in the rafters of the bunkhouses or under the floorboards. Often the discovery of the soil leads to the discovery of a tunnel.

Moling is suited to the smaller men. But even if he were shorter and slighter, James would have no interest in tunnelling. For one thing, he has decided that the Germans are simply playing with the prisoners, that they know all about the digging and wait until a tunnel is just a foot from the wire fence before exposing it. And for another thing, James has suddenly become interested in remaining inside the prison camp.

THE FOURTH side of the prison camp is a river. Across the river there is an old stone wall, and before the river there is a tripwire and a fence topped with barbed wire. Unlike the barren landscape of the camp proper, the river offers vegetation, some trees, and a little grass. The slight slope from the camp to the river makes it a pleasant spot to linger in the warmer months and a good place to go for those seeking some respite from the constant society of their fellow prisoners.

James Hunter was captured in the winter of 1940. When the season turns and spring has started to show itself, James comes down to the river at every opportunity. He stops bashing the circuit when he realizes that he has spent weeks walking the perimeter of the camp and the ground is now as grooved as a furrow from a succession of footsteps endlessly tamping down the earth. Now, in the evenings before the prisoners are locked in their barracks for the night, James comes instead to the fence near the river and stands under one of the three trees on the bank, watching the water roll slowly downstream, towards the town that he knows is there but will probably never see.

The river is perhaps ten feet across, the water tea coloured and not over a man's head. In the middle of the day, when the sun is directly above, James can see the rocks and sand on the bottom of the river, all of it murky through the sepia filter of the water's hue.

The volume of the river changes with the season. With spring it has widened, and all the rocks that protruded above the surface in winter are swallowed by the increase in volume. When the river flows deep and wide it is largely silent. When James first arrived at the camp, the river was barely a foot deep and it rattled with its own emptiness.

It is a fast-moving river. James has watched a leaf, blown onto the surface of the water, drift downstream and disappear around the bend before he has counted to thirty, the leaf moving at roughly one foot per second. The current is swifter in the spring, when the river is deep, the flex of the water more powerful.

At first, James thinks that he will make a study of the river, that it would be good to attach himself to a purpose while a prisoner in the camp. He doesn't want to dig useless tunnels, is not much interested in gardening or sport, prefers not to lie around in his bunk like Harry Stevens, waiting for the war to end. The men in the camp do not need him to teach them grammar school science, the only worthwhile skill he has on offer. The prison camp is filled with highly educated officers. In his bunkhouse alone, there are fourteen men who have been to either Oxford or Cambridge.

But the trouble with the river is that James has no real access to it. He can stand near the wire and watch the little bit of it that flows past the camp, but he cannot wade through it, examine the banks in detail, plunge his hand into the current to feel the temperature and pull of the water. He can visit it, but he will never know it. As a study, it will ultimately be inadequate and disappointing.

It is a warm spring day in 1940 when he thinks this, standing as close to the wire as he dares, feeling the breeze on his skin and watching it move the branches of the trees on the opposite shore.

It is in this exact moment that he hears the song of the bird and all his thoughts are silenced.

The beginning of something is easy to recall because it signals a change in direction. James Hunter came down to the river, which was one side of his prison, and he saw the redstarts on the stone wall, and the beauty of their song and the splash of red on their tails made him decide to study them for the length of time he was to be kept in the camp.

THE BIRDS were singing down by the river. Two redstarts on a grey stone wall. One was singing more beautifully and more often than its fellow, and James wondered then if some birds were simply better singers than others, and if this constant song was a rejoicing in their abilities.

The song of the redstart begins as a melody and ends in dissonance, as though the song itself comes undone in the process of singing it, finishing up with all the right notes presented in completely the wrong order.

James had no paper down by the river. He made no notes. He carried the memory of the song back up the hill to his small wooden desk in the bunkhouse, but when he sat down to write what he had heard, the words unravelled like the song of the bird, and he was left with nothing.

He returned to the river the next day. The male birds were still there, still singing and trying to attract a female. James realized that if he meant to watch them with purpose, he would need to document them. He would need to bring a notebook and pencil with him to the river and find a place to sit under a tree, as near to the wire as he could without drawing the attention of the guards.

In his room in the bunkhouse, James has secured a top bunk near the only window. None of the other men had wanted this spot because the window is drafty, but James doesn't mind suffering the cold in exchange for the opportunity to watch the changing sky and weather, or to feel the sun on his face in the afternoon because the window faces west.

The men in his flight crew have been allocated to different bunkhouses and different camps, and as they were never his friends, James doesn't miss them or seek them out. The seven other men in his room are nice enough fellows. They pool their Red Cross parcels so the food will stretch further, and they share books and jokes, but the only one of them to whom James is remotely close is the man who occupies the bottom bunk, Harry Stevens.

The second morning he observes the redstarts, James charges back up the slope to his room to get a notebook and pencil so he can begin documenting the birds. When he bursts through the door, Harry Stevens is lying on his bunk, reading a book. Stevens uses his books as a screen to avoid talking to his cabin mates, a trait that James understands, being often overwhelmed himself by constant human interaction. But sometimes he is disappointed when Harry chooses to use his book as a screen against him as well.

"There are redstarts by the river." James scrambles up the ladder to his bunk, where he keeps writing materials on a small shelf near his pillow.

"Red what?" Harry peers over the top of his novel.

"Birds. Two males. They're trying to attract females. I might get a breeding pair." James grabs a notebook and two pencils from the shelf. "I'm going to make a study of the redstarts. It will keep me busy here, and with luck, I can turn it into a book after the war."

"Best of British, then." Harry has already lost interest in James's pursuit. He turns a page of his novel. "Make sure you pull the door tight on your way out."

The deprivations of the Oflag make men's true natures rise to the surface fairly quickly, and what James had initially liked about Harry Stevens—his aloofness and polite reluctance at having too much to do with his fellow prisoners—has to be respected in every instance, even in circumstances where James would have preferred Harry to act a little more out of character.

THE BETTER singer of the male redstarts entices a female to join him, and it is not long before they start to build a nest together.

In the spring, when most of James's observations are taken, the days carry both promise and heartache. Often he shivers down by the river, and the birds huddle inside their feathered coats. On the days when it is sunny, they bask in the warmth together.

James had seen redstarts in Britain, but never a nesting pair. And back in that other life, which seems to fade more with each passing day, he didn't have much time to watch the world. He was too busy moving through it.

From his position near the fence, James can observe the redstarts building their nest in the stone wall across the river. They are about thirty feet away from him, near enough that he can make out most of the details of their courtship and nest building. He would love a pair of spyglasses, to observe their activity more closely, but spyglasses, for obvious reasons, are not permitted in camp.

The redstart nest is constructed with twigs and roots as its foundation. To this is added an insulating layer of dead grasses, feathers, wool scraps, animal hair, blanket threads, string, paper, moss, and what looks to be part of a bandage made of cotton wool.

The birds make use of what is on offer to them, which means they avail themselves of the prisoner's scraps, the evidence of life in the Oflag forming the foundation of their little home.

James watches the building of the nest for eleven straight hours, interrupted only once for roll call, and in those eleven hours the female redstart brings building materials to her nest a full 239 times.

The time it takes to build a nest and lay eggs varies from couple to couple, and much depends on the weather, as no bird likes to use wet materials to build a nest and so will wait out rain and inclemency. The redstart pair that James is watching is lucky in that it's dry for their nest building and so it takes them only four days to complete the task.

James doesn't know what observations will matter later, when he looks through his notes, so he writes everything down. In between the notations on the redstarts' activity, he writes larger questions about the birds' behaviour—questions he thinks about when he lies in his bunk at the end of the day.

Are some birds more strong-willed than their fellows? Do they push forward in times when other birds would wait? What is the greater imperative, I wonder, in all enterprises—desire or circumstance?

What is particular to the species in terms of the redstarts' behaviour, and what is a matter of individual temperament? Is it reasonable for this pair to represent all redstarts, when perhaps the necessity of being themselves is of more relevance than the fact that they are redstarts?

BEFORE LONG, James's vigil by the river is judged suspicious, and he is marched off between two guards to the Kommandant's office.

James has not been inside the German quarters before, and he is surprised to find them as barren as the bunkhouses. There is the same rudimentary wooden furniture scattered through the room. No rugs. No decorations on the walls. The walls themselves, being stone, make the Kommandant's office seem colder, and the lack of personal effects makes it appear a good deal grimmer than James's own room in bunkhouse 11.

The Kommandant rises from behind his desk when the prisoner is ushered into his office. He extends his hand and James shakes it solemnly, as though they were being introduced at a cocktail party.

"Please sit down," the Kommandant says. His English is very good, carries no trace of an accent.

James sits on the rickety wooden chair that faces the desk. He wonders if the Germans also have to periodically saw pieces off their furniture to feed the stove during the winter months.

The Kommandant is older than James by more than ten years; he's also plumper, with a receding hairline and pale-grey eyes. His brow is furrowed with lines, worry that has existed since before this war.

"You have been seen loitering by the river," he says. "Are you perhaps thinking of escaping?"

James is impressed with the word "loitering." This man has not learned English on the job, making simple translations from ordinary German words into ordinary English ones. The Kommandant has clearly come to this job already equipped with English.

"I'm not escaping," says James. "I'm watching the birds."

"*Der Vogel?*" The Kommandant seems surprised. Whatever lie he was expecting, this is not it.

"Redstarts." James produces his notebook from a jacket pocket. He hands it across the desk. "There is a breeding pair down by the river."

The Kommandant carefully turns the pages of the notebook, peering at James's cramped handwriting and his tiny pencil sketches.

"You are very thorough."

"I mean to make a proper study."

The Kommandant hands the notebook back across the desk to his prisoner.

"I will allow it, then," he says. "But only because you are making a proper study." He smiles, and James can't tell if he is mocking him or not.

"Thank you," he says, tucking the notebook back inside his jacket.

The guard opens the office door for him, and James steps out onto the wooden porch and then down onto the earth of the yard, still puzzling over the tone of the Kommandant's remark.

~~~

THERE'S A tunnel underway this spring, a big one, started in bunkhouse 14, which is near the centre of the camp, farther from the wire than the bunkhouses where other tunnels have been started. The tunnellers are hoping that this will throw the Germans off the scent, that it won't occur to them to be suspicious of one of the middle bunkhouses. The extra fifty feet they have to dig seems worth it if they are successful in fooling the guards.

One of the tunnellers is in James Hunter's room in bunkhouse 11. His name is Davis and he is known as the Modeller because he is making a scale model of the village where he used to live out of bits of wood, tin, and cardboard. Sometimes he solicits the Artist to help him decorate the facades of the tiny buildings. He keeps the finished pieces in a box under his bunk, but occasionally he'll display the village on the table in the middle of an afternoon, when most of the men are outside playing football or bashing the circuit.

"He moves the models around a lot," Harry said to James once. "As if he can't quite remember where the buildings actually go, even though he remembers what they look like."

All their activity is about not forgetting, thinks James, listening to the Modeller hum as he waits for the tinpot teakettle to boil. No one knows how long the war will last, and none of the men want to lose themselves in the process. By constructing the house they used to live in or lecturing on the subjects they once taught, they are able to hold on to the memory of the men they used to be. The unspoken hope for all of them is that when the war does end, they will be able to step back into those lives and continue on as though they'd never had to leave, and as though nothing of any consequence had happened to them in the war.

James leans over the edge of his bunk. The Modeller has his back to James, is sitting at the table working on assembling one of his miniature buildings. From his perspective, James can't tell what the building is going to be, but he can see from the hunch of Davis's body over his work how much attention he is paying to what he is doing.

When James had asked the Modeller why he was involved in digging the tunnel, Davis had just said, "I want to go home."

The effort that Ian Davis is taking in reconstructing, from memory, each stone of his childhood is touching, but James wonders if casting all one's attentions towards home is really the right approach to being a prisoner.

"It's coming along," he says. But Davis, intent on his task, doesn't reply, or doesn't hear him.

The roofs of the miniature buildings make James think that's how they would look to a bird flying over the real village.

Or an aeroplane.

He had joined the air force because James wanted the height and distance of the plane in relation to the ground. "So I don't have to see the people I'm killing," he had said to his sister, Enid, when she asked him why he'd chosen the RAF. "So I don't have to know that I've killed them."

AFTER THE nest is built, the clutch of eggs is laid. James can't tell how many eggs there are, but he can see that the base of the nest is covered in a light-blue colour, so there are probably as many as half a dozen.

When the chicks are born, their gullets are a bright orange. If the nest was dark or in the hollow of a tree, the adult redstarts would be able to see the bright throats of their babies and know where to place the food they have brought back to them.

The arrival of the chicks cheers James. He likes listening to their tiny cries, seeing the splash of orange in their open mouths. It excites him to think that he'll be there when they fledge. He doesn't mind counting the number of times the adult birds return to the nest with food, or watching them catch insects in the air above the river. He is attached to the progress of the redstart family and is eager for it to be successful. Most baby birds don't survive into adulthood. There are countless predators waiting to snatch them from the nest or grab them from the ground after their first wobbly flight.

A few days after the chicks are born, James leaves his post at the river to attend the evening roll call. As is his habit now, he first returns to his bunkhouse room to put the notebook and pencil away on the shelf by his pillow. He's a bit late coming back from the river; most of the men are out in the yard already, and even Stevens is gone from his bunk. James hurriedly climbs the ladder, placing his notebook and pencil on the shelf, and just as he's about to climb back down, he sees an object on his pillow. It's a book, wrapped carefully in brown paper. James pulls off the paper and sees a guidebook to the birds of Germany. The page with the entry on the redstart has a piece of paper placed there as a bookmark. Written on the paper, in neat script, are the words "To help you with your proper study of the birds."

"YORKSHIRE PUDDING," says Harry, "dripping with gravy. Fresh green beans from my father's allotment. Apple Charlotte to finish."

"Omelette," says James. "Mushroom and cheese, with a stack of toast and butter."

"Remember how good butter used to taste?" says Harry. "A little cool from being in the larder. Pale and creamy. Just the right amount of salt."

"A pint of ale," says James.

"Two pints of ale."

"A ham sandwich, with mustard and butter."

"We're back to butter again." Harry flicks his cigarette onto the earth at his feet. "Let's switch to people. Who do you miss the most?"

They're walking the circuit just before evening roll call. It's a warm spring evening. James is convinced he can smell apple blossoms on the breeze that wafts over the camp. As they pass the office, the door opens and the Kommandant steps out onto his wooden porch. He looks right at James and smiles.

"Who is it?" says Harry.

"What?"

"Who do you miss?"

James breaks eye contact with the Kommandant as he and Harry walk past the porch.

"My wife," he says.

"What's her name?"

"Rose."

"And is she?"

"Is she what?"

"As lovely as a rose?"

"I suppose so." James looks over his shoulder. The Kommandant is still standing on the wooden porch. In exactly fourteen minutes they will pass in front of him again. Will he smile a second time, or will he be gone?

"You don't sound very convinced."

"It's private. How I feel about my wife is private."

34

Harry snorts with laughter, slaps James on the shoulder. "Have you not noticed where you are?" he says. "There's nothing here that's private, old chum."

The prisoners obsess about their women back home. They talk about them endlessly, carry their letters around—sniffing at them to inhale the fading perfume that might still linger on the page. The Artist is kept busy drawing life-size portraits of wives and girlfriends from photographs. The portraits are tacked up on the walls beside the men's bunks.

The men who don't have wives or girlfriends talk about missing their dogs or the countryside where they grew up. All of them have something back home to fixate on while they are locked away in the camp.

James thinks about his wife as often as any man, but where the others are public with their feelings, he prefers to keep his to himself. His marriage is his business, he thinks. By keeping his feelings private, he keeps them active. The men who talk and talk about their wives are spending those feelings here, and when they get back to England, they might find that nothing of that emotion is left and their wives are now strangers to them.

HE'S NERVOUS knocking on the office door the next day. When the guard opens it, he doesn't know what to say about his reason for being there.

"Tell him that James Hunter is here," he says. And then, fearing that the Kommandant won't know who this is, he adds, "The Birdman."

The office is the same as it was the last time he was there. The Kommandant rises from behind his desk and shakes James's hand again. He says something in German to the two guards in the room and they both leave, closing the door quietly behind them.

"How can I assist you?" asks the Kommandant, sounding like a London shop clerk.

James takes the bird guide from his pocket and puts it on the desk.

"Thank you for your gift," he says. "But I don't read German."

"No, of course not." The Kommandant picks up the guide, opening it to the page with the bookmark. "Would you like me to read it to you? It is the redstart you are watching, correct?"

"Yes, it is. Yes, well, I suppose that might be helpful."

The Kommandant lays the book flat on the desk-top and clears his throat.

"It will help me to practise my English," he says. "To read to you."

"Your English is already very good," says James. He wants to ask why this is but feels that he'd be overstepping a boundary—although he guesses that boundary has already been overstepped by the Kommandant in choosing to read a German book aloud to a British prisoner.

The Kommandant reads slowly, carefully, never stumbling over words, but making sure he has enunciated each one before moving on to the next. His voice is deep and calming. James suddenly feels crashingly weary. He would like to topple off his chair and sleep for months on the stone floor of the office.

"The heart of the redstart beats at fourteen times the rate of a human heart," reads the Kommandant. "This is approximately 980 beats a minute." He looks over the top of the book. "So fast," he says, "it wouldn't beat so much as vibrate."

James says nothing, but he thinks that the fast heartbeat is likely the primary reason for the brief life of the bird. It simply uses itself up.

When the Kommandant finishes reading the redstart entry, he closes the book and pushes it towards James.

"You keep it," he says. "It will assist you with your German."

"But I don't need to learn German," says James.

"Yes, you do. It is going to be a long war, I think. You will be a guest in my country for a few years at least. Take the book."

James recognizes a command when he hears one, so he picks up the guidebook and stands up to leave. He hesitates before walking towards the door.

"Thank you," he says.

"You are welcome." The Kommandant also stands, and James notices how his uniform strains over his chest and stomach, as though it is one size too small or the Kommandant has increased one size while in charge of the camp. All the prisoners are losing weight, James thinks as he walks out of the dark office and into the sunny morning.

If it weren't for the Red Cross parcels, the prisoners in the Oflag would be starving. Twice a day the Germans provide a meal of black bread and a thin soup that is often just water with a couple of potatoes thrown into it. The Red Cross packages, which arrive every fortnight or so, contain jam, chocolate, tea, biscuits, sardines, meat rolls, and dried milk. Each parcel is also bound up with ten feet of string, and the string is employed to make brushes, hammocks, football nets, even wigs for the theatricals. Cigarettes come by separate post, each man receiving an allotment of fifty per week. The few prisoners who don't smoke, James among them, use their cigarettes to barter for foodstuffs.

Everything is made use of. Every scrap of material is put towards practical purpose. Even the tins that the food comes in are fashioned into mugs and pots after they have been emptied.

Food preoccupies the prisoners. They talk about it constantly. Lately, Harry and James have taken to playing the game where they each describe a perfect meal.

When James returns from the Kommandant's office, Harry is lying on his bunk, reading. He looks up when James enters the room.

"I've been thinking about chocolate cake," he says. "A really rich one, made with about a dozen eggs and a filling of cream and butter."

"It would make you sick if you had chocolate cake now," says James, sitting down at the table in the centre of the room. "You're not used to rich food anymore."

"What's got into you?" Harry says.

"Nothing."

James drums his fingers on the table. The German bird guide in his jacket pocket feels heavy as a brick.

"What do you think of the Kommandant?" he asks. "You know, as a person."

"Well, I don't really think of him as a person," says Harry. He pauses. "I don't *want* to think of him as a person, I suppose. He's a Jerry. The guards are Goons. After the war, I won't give any of them another thought. After the war, when I'm eating a slice of that delicious chocolate cake." He is persistent, if nothing else, but James ignores his invitation.

"What do you think you'll do after the war?" asks James.

"Oh, I don't know," says Harry irritably. He picks up his book where it lies open on his chest. "Perhaps"—he brightens—"I'm reading so many novels that I might try my hand at one. How hard can it be?"

THAT NIGHT there is a debate in the bunkhouse, in the room at the end of the building. A debating society is one of the many diversions created by the prisoners of war to pass the time.

"Are you coming?" asks James at eight o'clock, after supper and evening roll call.

Harry lowers his novel to his chest. "What is the topic tonight?" he asks.

"Town life versus country life."

Harry yawns, and then stretches his arms overhead. "That doesn't interest me enough," he says. "You go on."

"But you haven't been to one yet," says James.

"Well, have I missed anything?"

James doesn't quite know how to answer, as it's true that none of the debates so far have been particularly riveting.

"Exactly," says Harry, and he picks up his novel and goes back to reading.

Because the captured officers are not required to work, there is a long stretch of day to fill between roll calls, and some of the entertainments devised to stave off boredom are not always wildly successful. James hasn't made his mind up about the debating society, but he has decided that if tonight's debate isn't lively enough, he won't return for next week's discussion on amateurs versus professionals.

The room where the debate is to take place is overcrowded; people spill out into the hallway. James leans up against the doorframe to watch.

There are three men on each team. The structure of the event is for each of the men to give an introductory statement and then for the debate to begin after that. But the crowded room isn't conducive to listening, and the audience jostles and calls out during the opening remarks. What was meant to be an invigorating discussion on culture versus nature degenerates into name-calling and laughter.

"That was quick," says Harry, when James comes back to their room. "You've only been gone about twenty minutes."

"It was rubbish. No one would follow the rules."

"Perhaps everyone is just a little tired of rules."

"Perhaps." James climbs up onto his bunk and lies on his back with his hands behind his head, staring at the ceiling. The room is empty except for Harry and him. Everyone is down the hall.

"You're on the side of country life, aren't you?" says Harry.

"Yes."

"And you would never be convinced to live in a town?"

"No."

"Then you've missed nothing."

"I'm sure there's more to it than that," says James. He listens to Harry turning a page of his novel, the sound, in the quiet of the room, vaguely reminiscent of wind in the tops of trees. "There would be a lot of arguing back and forth. Point and counterpoint."

"But you would never allow your mind to be changed," says Harry. "So there is no reason to listen to the arguments."

James agrees, but he doesn't say so out loud.

Harry seems to have heard anyway. "We're a debating society of two, James," he says. "And I've just won that one."

THE NEXT morning, James is sharpening pencils with Harry's pocketknife at the table in their bunk-house. He likes to have at least two spare pencils with him when he is at his post by the river, in case his working pencil breaks or wears down to wood. He carefully scrapes the body of the pencil, pushing the shavings into a small pile to give to Davis later. Davis likes to use them as roof tiles for the houses in his miniature village.

There's shouting out in the yard. German voices and then English voices yelling back.

James climbs the ladder of his bunk so he can look out the window.

"What is it?" says Harry from his own bunk.

A man is being dragged by two of the German guards across the compound towards an automobile at the camp gate. James can see smoke pluming out the exhaust of the waiting car. The engine is running. A small crowd of prisoners is following the guards and the captive.

"They're taking someone," James says.

"Who?"

"I can't tell from here."

James watches as the prisoner is shoved into the back seat of the motor car. One of the guards gets in after him. Then the Kommandant, who must have been standing on his porch, watching the whole procedure, steps down and climbs into the front seat of the car.

"Maybe he's being moved to a different camp," says James.

Harry snorts. "Don't tell me you believe that lie they're always telling us."

James does believe it, but it's clear from Harry's reaction that he shouldn't, so he says nothing.

The camp gate opens and the motor car drives slowly through. The crowd of prisoners starts to disperse.

"They're probably taking the poor sod out to be shot," says Harry.

"What for?"

"Does it matter? For anything. Or nothing. Don't be deceived, James. We're their prisoners and they can do what they like to us. We're not protected. The Geneva Conventions don't guarantee our safety. The Goons can breach those any time they choose."

THE BABY redstarts grow bigger and more demanding. They are constantly hungry, their cries louder, more plaintive every day. The adult birds forage for food during all available daylight hours. After the parents deliver the worm or flying insect or caterpillar to the chicks, they fly away from the nest with an energetic spurt, which James feels can only be relief. For a moment they are free of their duties—but only for a moment. After the little kick of freedom, they are back to the onerous task of finding fresh food to feed the inexhaustible chicks, which, it seems, are perpetually hungry.

The birds have become used to his presence, or they've learned to ignore it. James can't decide which it is. They have their routines, the birds and him, and James likes to think that the redstarts are not influenced by his surveillance, but simply continue on with their lives in ignorance of his. But he knows this is probably not the case, and he has to add into his research the factor of himself. To what extent his presence alters the birds' behaviour, he cannot know, but it is safe to assume that there is some alteration of their habits, and even though they become accustomed to James, they do not necessarily prefer that he is there, watching them.

〜〜〜

Aside from the delivery of the Red Cross packages, the most highly anticipated event is the arrival of the post. Every fortnight or so, James receives a letter from his parents telling him their news. None of it is particularly interesting or relevant to him, but he is always reassured by their descriptions of the English weather and the announcement of what is currently growing in their little garden. It is comforting to think of his parents' lives continuing on as usual, or at least their presenting it to him as though this is the case.

Occasionally James's wife, Rose, writes to him, her letters sometimes now weeks apart. She used to write much more regularly, and even though the content of her letters hasn't changed, James worries about the gap between them. Rose always begins her letter by apologizing for this, but he is not entirely convinced by her claims of busyness. She has her war job, the hens, and her Victory Garden, but there should still be enough time left over to write her husband a letter every day. He receives more letters from his sister, Enid, than he does from his wife.

The letter James receives from Rose today is all about her work as a blackout warden. She has taken on this job since his capture, walking the streets of their village and cautioning the inhabitants about the chink in their curtains that allows the light from their houses to bleed out into the thick country dark.

Rose writes about what she sees through the windows of the houses, and James imagines that she stands for a while in the road, watching, before she taps on the front door to issue her warning.

She writes her letters to him in the present tense, as though she is relaying what she is seeing just as it occurs in front of her.

I envy those who think of their lives to the exclusion of all else, she writes. *It would be so good to forget about the war, even for an instant.*

James reads his wife's letter down at the river, on duty watching the redstarts. He reads in snatches, a sentence or two, before looking up to keep track of the adult birds as they return to the nest with food for their babies.

Mr. Sandler fiddles with the knobs on the wireless in his lounge. He kneels down in front of the machine, his ear turned to the speaker as he twiddles with the tuning, trying to get perfect reception for the evening's programs. From where I stand in the garden, it looks like he is praying. Across the room, Mrs. Sandler looks up from her knitting and speaks to her husband, but I can tell that Mr. Sandler isn't listening to his wife at all and wishes she would just shut up so he can concentrate on the more important task of tuning the wireless. He never once turns towards her voice, just presses his ear harder against the speaker.

A bird flies into the nest with a caterpillar, remaining there for exactly ten seconds and then flying out again with that little kick of relief that James is used to by now. He wishes he had a view into the nest and could see if the caterpillar was given to one of the babies or was portioned out to all.

I stand outside the Crofters' cottage, watching sixteen-year-old Daisy dancing by herself in the front room, swaying to music that I can't hear. It is almost as though Mr. Sandler's wireless program has skipped down the row of cottages and ended up in Daisy's sitting room.

Rose and James had been married for only six months when James was captured. They have no children. Rose, in her husband's absence, has got herself a dog named Harris; she accompanies Rose on the nightly blackout rounds and sometimes makes an appearance in her letters.

It's a cool evening, the moon not yet up and the darkness thick as fog; a twisty wind conspires in the tops of the trees. Harris has gone ahead to look under Mr. Shepherd's hedge, where she once flushed a partridge, and then she heads farther down the road to the low wall, where she's hopeful there will be a cat to chase.

The dog makes James a little anxious because Rose never discussed it with him first. She just went ahead and got the dog, saying to James that she needed the company, and that James would like Harris. While this may be true, and while James has nothing against the fact that Rose wanted a dog, it still makes him uneasy that she didn't think it necessary to consult him first. As husband and wife, they've spent almost as many months apart as together, and he could be in the camp for years yet, if the Kommandant is to be believed. He worries that instead of holding him fast in her memory, Rose is forgetting her husband and getting too used to a life without him.

The war has taken its toll on love. At least once a week, one of the men in the camp receives a letter from his beloved saying that she has left him for another. To deal with the crushing blow that these letters level, the prisoners have developed a system to help the abandoned lover address his grief. The Dear John letter is pinned to one of the communal bulletin boards so that everyone in the camp can read it. The public aspect of this gesture takes away some of the private grief suffered by the individual, and so the message of the letter ceases to be as powerful to its recipient.

James is always a little afraid of receiving one of these letters, and this is another reason why he wants to fashion a new thread of discussion in his correspondence with his wife. He doesn't want his words home to degenerate into a litany of complaint—or worse yet, into self-pitying need. He wants it to seem as though the camp does not exist at all, as though he is writing to Rose what he would have written to her from anywhere. The letters do not depend on his being a prisoner. He is convinced, having seen enough Dear John letters on the bulletin board, that the secret to not being left is always to have something novel to offer his wife, even at this great distance and under these trying circumstances. The natural world is one of the things they had in common. Even though James and Rose had met in the city, they deliberately chose to live in the country because they both loved the countryside and wanted to spend their free time walking on the heath. They enjoyed the proximity to nature allowed by their little cottage on the edge of the Ashdown Forest.

James writes to Rose every week, trying always to be upbeat, cheerful. He works on his latest letter at the table in his bunkhouse room.

Dearest Rose, I have had the good fortune to have found a nest of redstarts and have decided to observe them for the duration of my stay here.

He never mentions the camp or the conditions. This is partly because he is afraid of the censor's hand. It is impossible to talk about events at the camp in any detail to those on the outside. Last year the prisoners had a good laugh over a letter from Richard Hatton to his grandmother that was returned to him as undeliverable. A particularly enthusiastic censor had blacked out the whole letter, leaving only the salutation and the closing. *Dear Granny, Love Richard.*

James fears the censor, but he also wants to spare Rose any of his suffering. He has never been much of a complainer, and it seems proper to protect his wife from his reality and concentrate instead on information that will be cheering to her. He doesn't say that the redstarts are on the other side of the barbed wire. He writes instead, *I keep a good distance from the birds so that they will not be too disturbed by my presence.*

Halfway through the letter, James has the inspiration to suggest to Rose that she find a nest of redstarts in England to watch, and that way, by studying the birds with the same degree of concentration as her husband, she would keep him company at his task and they would not really be separated at all. They could share their findings and it would help him make a better study. Her findings might echo his.

Harry Stevens passes behind James on his way to the stove to make tea. He reads over his friend's shoulder.

"Damn and blast," he says. "It's all about the bloody birds."

James covers his letter with a hand. "Rose likes to know what I'm doing at the camp," he says. "How I'm spending my time."

Harry moves away from the table and towards the stove. "I doubt that," he says.

"How can you be an expert on marriage when you're not married?"

"That is precisely what makes me an expert." Harry roots through the used tea bags in a tin on top of the stove to find one that has a little bit of life left in it. "Ask yourself this, Hunter—if you were a woman, wouldn't you rather receive a letter filled with lovemaking than descriptions of some bloody bird's nest?"

"You may feel you're an expert on marriage, but you're not an expert on *my* marriage." James lifts his hand and starts back in to his letter to Rose, but he feels a little worm of doubt from Stevens's words wriggle into his head and settle there.

THE CRIES of the baby redstarts grow stronger every day. It won't be long before they fledge, and this also makes James nervous. He feels confident about their safety while they are in the nest, but once they leave it, their survival becomes much more difficult. They will no longer be protected by their parents, or by the excellent location of their nest. Instead they will be out in the larger world, which is full of predators and danger.

In his other life, back home, James had often walked by young birds stumbling around on the grass, not knowing enough to move quickly out of his way in case he meant them harm. The period before something learns to be afraid is the most dangerous period of all, because it is then that creatures are the most vulnerable.

First the redstart chicks have to learn to be afraid. Then they must learn to be aggressive towards smaller birds. And finally they will learn to be aggressive towards intruders of their own species so they can defend their families.

ON THE day that he receives Rose's latest letter, James sees a swarm of bees over the river. He actually hears them before he sees them—a raspy noise that is not one continuous hum, but rather the sound of overlapping buzzing, like an engine that is frantically sparking but failing to catch.

The swarm is hovering over the river, a swirling mass of thousands of bees stirring the air. They are closer together as a group at the centre of the swarm, and there are single bees on the outside of the mass—scouts, perhaps, trying to decide in which direction to guide the group. These loose bees make the swarm look as though it is unravelling.

James stands very still. He doesn't want the bees to see him. He is afraid of being stung. But the bees don't seem interested in his presence, or that of the birds in the stone wall. They are not even interested in their own flight. They are looking for a place to land. One of the scout bees moves downriver and the swarm follows, flying in a thick, circular motion above the water, and then out over the trees and away.

JAMES WRITES a note about the swarm that evening, after roll call. He writes his notes every evening, sitting at his little desk between two sets of bunk beds. The bee swarm hasn't anything to do with the redstarts, but because it happened in their territory, James feels that he should make note of it. He is meticulous in this regard, trying to observe everything in the vicinity of the redstart nest and taking a written record of it, just in case it comes to matter later, when he assembles his notes into a book.

Davis comes over to him while he's writing and puts the cardboard box with his model village on James's desk.

"The tunnel's nearly done," he says. "We're going soon. If I get away, could you post this to my parents at the end of the war? I've written their address on the top of the box."

"You want me to do this?" asks James. He stops short of asking why. He and Davis are collegial with each other, but they aren't friends.

"Yes. Because you're here for the duration," says Davis. "I can depend on that."

James accepts this answer to his unasked question and turns in his chair to face the younger man. "Are you sure you want to go? You'll most likely be caught. You could even be shot."

Davis shrugs. "I don't want to be here," he says.

"But you are here," says James.

"Not for much longer."

It suddenly seems to James that the camp is divided between men like Davis, who feel it is their duty to try to escape because they long to be elsewhere, and men like him, who make the best of where they are by investing their time in purposeful activities. James looks at the bold printing on the lid of the box. Davis is only twenty. He has parents rather than a wife. His childhood must still be so near to him, so familiar.

"I'll take care of it," he says.

"I knew I could count on you," says Davis. "You're the most reliable chap in camp."

Later that night, everyone in James's room goes to another of the bunkhouse rooms to join a card game. There's only James and Harry left behind. As they often do, they lie in their bunks, chatting and falling silent. It is an odd feeling to talk to someone without seeing him, but James is used to it now and finds it reassuring to hear Harry's deep voice rising up to him from the bottom bunk, where his friend lies reading. The Red Cross has sent another shipment of books to the camp, and the prisoners have started a lending library. Harry uses the library on a daily basis, and even though there are a few thousand volumes now, James wouldn't be surprised if Harry makes his way through all the books by next Christmas, and it is already almost June.

"Do you think they'll make it?" James says, meaning Davis and the other dozen tunnellers.

"One of these days someone's bound to get away," says Harry. "But no, I don't think it will be them. Not this time. Tunnels take too long. They're too risky. The Goons probably already know about it."

"I wish he wouldn't go. He's so young."

"You're a bit of a mother hen, James."

"I don't want him to get shot." James thinks how awful it will be if he has to post the model village to Davis's parents because their son has been killed while escaping. It will be a macabre object for them to receive in the post.

"Mostly the tunnellers are not shot," says Harry. "Mostly they're rounded up by the dogs and hauled back to camp, where they're thrown into the cooler for a few weeks. Made an example of for the rest of us miserable sods. All their hard work for nothing. The tunnels get filled back up again. Escaping seems just as much a hobby as your birds or Hickson's golf course." He shifts and the frame of the bunk bed wobbles. "I'm going to read now, James," he says. "Try to stop worrying."

James lies in his bunk, his hands behind his

head, staring up at the darkened wooden ceiling. I wish I were a bird, he thinks. In the forest, perched in the trees at the edge of the river, flying over the water at dusk. He would feel the heat of the sun on the stone wall or the cool of evening's shadow. He could lift and lower at will, rise over the wire, into the sky beyond the forest, above the war itself. He could soar higher than the planes. He could take himself home.

HICKSON, KNOWN as the Golfer, in bunkhouse 2, is constructing a golf course at the camp. He comes to see James at the river the next morning, charging down the slope like a bull after cows.

"Hunter," he bellows, so loudly that James starts like the birds he's watching, dropping his pencil on the ground.

Hickson is brawny and big. He is a champion athlete at the camp, always on the winning side at football and cricket. Even though James doesn't know him well, he imagines that Hickson was very much the same back in England. He knew such boys at school, heavily involved in sport and relentlessly popular. And now, after tiring of practising his putting outside his bunkhouse, Hickson has got it into his head that he wants to construct a nine-hole golf course in the camp.

Hickson slides to a stop beside James.

"Hunter," he says, "I am in need of your opinion."

"About birds?" asks James.

"No, no. About here." Hickson surveys the little bit of ground around them. "In your opinion, would this be a spot of rough, or could I transform it into hole number seven?"

"Rough," says James without any hesitation at all, because if it's rough, then it will have less human traffic than a proper stop on the course. "The ground's very uneven through here, and there are these tree roots." He kicks at one to give an illustration. There are only a few trees growing by the river, and the roots really wouldn't be much of an impediment at all, but James does not want a golf course right in the midst of his observation area. It would make the redstarts nervous and possibly scare them away for good.

"Interesting." Hickson cocks his head to one side and then the other as he regards the tree root.

"Oh, look at that beauty." He bends down and picks something from the ground, stands up, and opens his hand to show James the pebble that lies there.

"A rock?" says James.

"A golf ball," says Hickson. He tosses the pebble gently into the air, catches it, tosses it again. "The centre of the golf ball, to be more precise. It's weighted perfectly. Now I'll wrap it with twine and then cover it with leather from one of the old footballs. I'm learning to stitch like a seamstress," he says, grinning at James. "You'll have to come and have a go when the course is done."

"Yes," says James, although he has no intention of golfing. Watching his redstarts is a full-time job. "Will this be rough, then?"

Hickson has moved his attention from the tree root to the pebble. He's still tossing it up and down in the air. "If you think so," he says. "I defer to your expertise."

James watches him charge back up the slope, full of purpose and on to his next task. He is perhaps more dedicated to his pursuit of sport than James is to his redstarts, and that thought cheers James. Even though Hickson is the sort of person James steered clear of in civilian life, they are on the same side here in the camp. They are both attaching themselves to life here rather than seeking to escape from it. They are both, as Ian Davis put it, here for the duration.

THE GARDENER works the patch of ground in front of his bunkhouse. From the sandy soil he is trying to coax lettuce, tomatoes, onions, carrots, as well as dahlias, chrysanthemums, and tulips. He is but one of many gardeners in the camp. The vegetables they are able to cultivate will be welcome additions to the food the prisoners receive in the Red Cross parcels, and for this reason, gardening is popular among the men. Vegetable and flower seeds are sent via the Red Cross, and the Royal Horticultural Society back in Britain has even allowed POWs to sit gardening exams so that, after the war, they may find employment doing what, during the war, was undertaken out of necessity.

The Gardener has sat the exam and received his qualifications in absentia. Although a trained geologist, he told James that he preferred gardening now, and that he couldn't imagine not preferring it when he resumed civilian life again.

When James isn't at the river watching the red-starts, he likes to sit on the steps of bunkhouse 2 and watch the Gardener work his little plot of soil. It is heartening to see the vegetables and flowers take their shape through the spring, rising up towards maturity under the Gardener's careful ministrations.

There is more than one garden outside bunk-house 2 and more than one gardener at work when James drops by to drink his mug of afternoon tea on the steps. There are two other prisoners in their small plots. One of the men James does not know well, but the other is Carmichael, a tall, lanky fellow, awkward at sport but skilled at persuading the poor soil of his plot to yield an astonishing array of vegetables. He's whistling softly as he hoes a row of onions.

James waves to Carmichael and drops down on the steps of the bunkhouse.

"Have you given the birds a tea break too?" asks the Gardener, straightening up from his work of hilling the beans.

"I take my break at a different time each day," says James. "That way I can know what's happening when I'm not there. The redstarts have a routine. They don't vary it much."

"Like all of us," says the Gardener. He comes over and sits down on the steps beside James. "Give me a mouthful, Hunter."

James passes his tin-can mug of tea to his friend.

The bunkhouses are numbered according to their proximity to the Kommandant's office; the smaller numbers are those closest to it. From the steps of bunkhouse 2, James has a good view of the Kommandant's office window, and he's surprised, when he looks up at it, to see the Kommandant looking back at him.

The Gardener passes the tin can back to James.

"I'd prefer the birds to Carmichael," he says. "He's been whistling that same bloody tune for hours now."

James cocks his head to the side and hears the short, familiar musical phrase that he can't quite place begin its loop again. And in that moment, when he tilts his head to listen, the German guard who is standing against the wall of the bunkhouse not twenty feet away unbuttons the holster of his Luger, walks up to Carmichael, and shoots him through the temple.

~~~

THE NEXT morning, James is back at his post at the river when two guards rush down the slope towards him.

"Mitkommen!" one of them says, grabbing James by the arm and pulling him up the rise.

He can't think what he has done, why the Kommandant would want to see him again. But James is not taken to the Kommandant's office. He is led to the main gates of the camp and to a large black sedan parked there.

One of the guards pushes James into the back seat of the motor car and climbs in after him. The other guard gets into the driver's seat. The engine starts up, the gates of the camp open, and the car moves out onto a bumpy stretch of country road. It is only then, as they are leaving the camp, that James sees that the person in the front passenger seat is the Kommandant.

"Where are you taking me?" James asks, the panic rising in his throat.

But none of the men in the car answer, or even look at him. They are all staring ahead at the road, which twists slowly through the fields.

James is sweating. He rubs his face with his

sleeve. He is restless with agitation, his foot tapping against the floor of the car.

"I haven't done anything," he says.

The Kommandant turns around. "Try to relax," he says. "Try not to worry."

And then James knows for certain that he is going to be executed. He leans his head against the car window, the glass cool against his temple. The little picture he keeps at the back of his mind of Rose and his cottage on the edge of the Ashdown Forest dissolves into fear. He can't reach it for comfort now.

The road, little more than a lane, is bumpy and rutted. The car makes slow progress through the fields. James has no sense of time, cannot judge how far they have driven. The moments he is in the car are both horribly short and horribly long.

The landscape gradually alters. Where once there were fields stretching out on either side of the motor car, now there are only woods. Northern woods of pine and fir, the trees growing so closely together that there is no light visible between the trunks.

They pull off the road and lurch to a stop.

"*Aussteigen!*" says the guard in the back seat beside James. He nudges him with his arm.

"Get out," translates the Kommandant. "Please."

James exits the car. For a brief moment he considers making a dash for it, but the field extends for quite a way before it reaches the edge of the trees. He would be shot almost immediately. It would be worse to be shot in the back, perhaps, than to be made to kneel in the middle of a field and take a bullet through the temple.

"Now we walk," says the Kommandant. He leads them across the field. The two guards flank James. They all trudge across the stiff grass and enter the woods. They will shoot me here, then, thinks James, and leave my body hidden among the trees, where it won't be seen from the road.

If these are to be his last moments on earth, he wants to savour them. He wants to be able to concentrate on the smoky light coming down through the trees, the damp patches of moisture on the ground as they move deeper into the woods. But all James can do is listen to the sticky tattoo of his blood in his veins, the stutter of his heart. He can feel the sweat running down his chest. There is no world outside the noise of his own body in this moment.

The Kommandant holds up his hand and every-one sways to a stop.

"Why?" says James, but the Kommandant, who has turned to face the prisoner, holds a finger to his lips. Then he moves the finger from his lips, and James thinks that the Kommandant is about to kill him, that he will unbutton the leather holster at his hip and remove the Luger that sits there, tell James to kneel on the ground, and put a bullet through his head.

But the Kommandant removes the finger from his lips and points into the air above them.

"Look," he says. "Look up there."

James tilts his head back and directs his gaze to where the Kommandant's hand is pointing. Up at the top of a fir tree there are a dozen or so birds balanced on the branches, chattering to one another.

"Cedar waxwings," says the Kommandant. "Here by accident, do you think?"

James looks dumbly at the birds.

"They are not common to these parts," continues the Kommandant. "They are what I think you would call an *accidental*."

"Yes." James looks at the sleek waxwings at the top of the fir tree. He has seen these birds in his reference books, but never in person before. Sometimes there are Bohemian waxwings in Britain, but never cedar waxwings. "Vagrants or accidentals. Often blown off their migratory routes by a storm."

"In German we call these birds *Seidenschwänze*," says the Kommandant. "It means 'silken tails.'"

The waxwings are neatly groomed, their feathers slicked back as though with pomade.

The Kommandant waves his hand at the guards and speaks to them sharply in German. They retreat through the trees. James listens to their footsteps crisping through the leaves on the forest floor.

"I sent them away so we could talk freely," says the Kommandant.

The waxwings chirp from the top of the tree, their overlapping sounds buoyant and cheerful.

"I thought you were going to kill me," James says.

The Kommandant looks stricken. "No, no," he says. "I just wanted to surprise you. I meant no harm." He reaches out and touches James on the shoulder. "I wanted to stop the war, just for the morning, so we could enjoy the birds together. We are not so different, you and I."

"In some ways, no," James says. "But you can kill me if you choose, and I can do nothing to stop it." He pauses, feeling his heartbeat gradually return to normal. "Your English is very good."

"I lived in England."

"When?"

"I went to Oxford. After the first war." The Kommandant takes a cigarette case from the pocket of his coat. He opens it and offers it to James.

"Thank you, but I don't smoke."

The Kommandant withdraws a cigarette from the case, clicks the silver box shut, and returns it to his coat pocket. He lights a match, cupping his hand around the flame. James notices that the older man's hand is shaking slightly.

"What did you read at Oxford?" he asks.

"Classics. I teach at the University of Berlin. Like you, I am not a soldier."

How odd, thinks James, that this war and the last have been fought by classics professors and bird-watchers, gardeners and watercolourists.

"Christoph." The Kommandant extends his hand and James shakes it.

"James."

"Do you like the *Seidenschwänze*, James?"

"They're very beautiful."

The smoke from the Kommandant's cigarette rises up through the tight canopy of trees. James watches it dissolve in the cool morning air.

"I lived in your country," says the Kommandant. "For many years. Before I went to Oxford, I was a prisoner of war and worked on a farm. That's where I learned my good English."

"You fought in the first war?"

"I was a boy then and knew nothing of fighting. I thought the war would be an adventure."

"A terrible adventure, I imagine."

"Yes. For days, I fought on while all the men in my trench were dead or wounded. Finally the English soldiers simply walked across the muddy stretch of ground between their trenches and ours, and took me prisoner. One of the soldiers gave me some choc- olate. I had been surviving on water. They called me a hero for holding the line, but really I was just too afraid to move."

Christoph takes a pull on his cigarette.

"But working on the farm was very soothing. I liked the rhythm of tending to the animals. My time was attached to their needs. It made the days bearable." He pauses. "How is your bird study progressing?"

"It's going well," says James. "I've logged a lot of hours watching the redstarts. The chicks are about to fledge. I worry for their safety when they leave the nest."

"Yes, of course. It's very difficult to survive in this world." The Kommandant finishes his cigarette, stamps it out in the earth. "We should go back now. It is not a good idea for me to talk to you for very long."

The guards are leaning up against the sedan car. James can see them there as he and the Kommandant step out of the woods and start across the field. There's an ease to the guards when the Kommandant isn't around, in the way they slouch against the hood of the motor car, smoking. Their laughter spools like birdsong through the air towards him.

"They behave as men on a break from their jobs. They are not real soldiers either. One of them was a baker. The other worked on the railway." The Kommandant sighs. "It might be a long war," he says, "that we are all waiting out together. It might be a long time before Weber makes a loaf of bread again."

The drive back to the camp is no different from

the drive out, but James feels such relief at not having been shot that it translates into a sort of ecstatic happiness. He presses his face to the window and watches the countryside shudder past. The fields are just now emerging from their long winter sleep, the brown grass tipped green in patches, the sun pooling on the surface. He is suddenly touched by the Kommandant's gesture of friendship, and cheered by the sight of the waxwings in the fir tree. It has been a most extraordinary morning. He must find some way to tell Rose about it.

When they arrive back in camp, he hurries down to the river to check on the redstarts. As he waits by the fir where he usually stands to survey the birds, he realizes that something is wrong. There is no activity around the stone wall across the river. Where only yesterday the adult redstarts came to the nest with food every few minutes, now there is no sign of the birds. The chicks have fledged while he was away with the Kommandant. And where baby birds in the nest do nothing but make noise—to persuade their parents to feed them—adolescent birds that have left the nest must remain perfectly silent for fear of attracting predators. The baby redstarts will be hiding in the trees and bushes near the stone wall, trying not to draw attention to themselves, but from this moment on they will be invisible to James, no matter how quiet he is or how much he watches. The young birds must stay hidden now in order to survive into adulthood. They will call out from their hiding places, and their parents will bring them food. Then, after a week or two, they must find new territory to occupy. They must find their own food.

James misses the chicks with a ferocity that surprises him. He is anxious for their survival and upset that he has missed his chance of seeing them. All these weeks of waiting and he still doesn't know how many babies were actually in the nest.

THAT EVENING after curfew, when they are locked in their bunkhouses for the night, James lies awake in his bed, listening to the chatter of the other men in the room and thinking about his childhood on the farm. He remembers the dogs and the thick soup of mud in the yard, the warmth of the kitchen stove, the outline of the sheep on the hills at dusk. He remembers his mother with newly hatched chicks in her apron pocket, to keep them warm after they had the misfortune to be born during the cold winter months. And he remembers the birds—the kestrels over the fields; the sparrows near the house; the geometry of the swallows outside his bedroom window, and the way they cut and parcelled the air into shapes with the blades of their wings. The lifting/falling sensation of the birds crossing in front of the mullioned windows, so like the rise and fall of his own breath.

As a boy, James studied the field guides with their black-and-white illustrations of birds. It was always startling to see the colour on the real birds when he came across them on his rambles in the countryside. Perhaps this is why he was so drawn to the redstarts, he thinks. Not just because they were available to him here at the camp, but because of the dramatic splash of red on their tail feathers, how the brightness of it astonished and cheered him every time he saw it.

"Where did you go this morning?" Harry's voice rises up from the bottom bunk and interrupts James's reverie.

"The Gardener saw you getting into the

Kommandant's sedan. Did they take you out to interrogate you about the tunnel?"

"No," says James. "Actually, the Kommandant brought me to a forest to see some cedar waxwings."

Harry snorts. "I'm not an idiot, Hunter. But if you don't want to talk about it, that's fine. As long as you didn't give anything away."

James does want to talk about the waxwings in the tops of the pine trees, wants to convince Harry, with the details of the morning, that he isn't lying. But perhaps it is better that his story is so unbelievable, because there is danger in his friendship with the Kommandant. He doesn't want to be seen as a collaborator by his fellow prisoners.

"I didn't give anything away," he says.

A WEEK after James was taken to see the cedar waxwings, Davis and the other tunnellers, having waited until after morning roll call, lift a wooden lid covered with earth, drop one by one through the trap door in the floor of bunkhouse 14, and begin their crawl to freedom.

They make it out of the camp. The Germans, it appears, did not know of their enterprise. That evening at roll call, their disappearance is discovered and there is a scramble by the guards to get after them with the dogs.

All night long, James lies in his bunk and hears the barking of the Alsatians. The prisoners in his room are silent, each man lying awake, willing the escapees through the woods, down into the town and onto a train, and then off the train again once safely in Switzerland. No one speaks. Their room in bunkhouse 11 practically vibrates with their combined prayers.

The escapees are captured the following day. While the prisoners are standing for evening roll call, the gates of the camp open and the men are dragged back inside the compound. Their clothes are ripped. One of the tunnellers has blood on his face from a gash above his left eye. They are pushed across the prison yard, made to pass in front of the men on parade on their way to the cooler, where they will be locked in solitary confinement for weeks as punishment. For all the individual industry in the camp, there is nothing to do in the cooler. No company or conversation. The long hours of solitude and inactivity carve into the soul of a man and alter him. The prisoner who gets thrown into the cooler after an escape is not the same man who returns to camp society after a month of being locked away.

"There are only eleven of them," whispers the Gardener, who is standing beside James. "Thirteen went through that tunnel. Perhaps two managed to get away?"

"Davis is missing." James feels his heartbeat increase at the thought that his young cabin mate has managed to escape.

But at the end of the line of the eleven living prisoners are four guards, two on either side of the two remaining men. The guards are dragging the prisoners by the arms. The prisoners are not moving. One of them is Ian Davis.

"Bastards," says Harry.

The guards drop the dead men at the foot of the porch in front of the Kommandant's office. Davis has been shot in the forehead. The other man has been shot through the chest. James feels bile rising in his throat and chokes to keep it down.

The Kommandant stands on his porch while the living escapees are dragged off towards the stone building that is used as the camp jail. He doesn't say anything, just watches with the rest of them as the captured prisoners are hauled away. James notices that the Kommandant avoids looking down at the dead men lying on the ground at his feet. He says nothing at all during the whole event. It is the adjutant, a thin, jittery man with a permanent angry expression, who yells out at the assembled prisoners.

"See! This is what happens if you try to escape. There is no escape. You will not escape. This is what happens."

No one likes the adjutant. He seems half crazy and operates at a fever pitch, always yelling and stamping around.

The Kommandant turns and walks back into his office. James thinks that perhaps he doesn't like the adjutant either, or the killing of the prisoners.

"Were they running?" he whispers to Harry. "Didn't they stop when the guards yelled?"

"They weren't running," says Harry. He spits in the earth at their feet. "They were shot in the front, not the back. Executed."

Were they shot simply to send a message to the rest of the prisoners? Was Ian Davis's life worth nothing more than that? James has the uneasy feeling that perhaps the Germans did know of this new tunnel after all, and that the entire episode was staged for the benefit of this warning, the opportunity for the guards to kill some Allies.

THE DEAD men are buried outside the wire, the mounded earth of their grave visible from James's bunkhouse window. He tries not to notice it every time he looks out the window—tries to focus on the sky, the clouds—but it is always there, in the bottom corner of every scene, a heavy underscore to the drifting clouds or the upright slashes of the pines.

Ian Davis's bunk is not yet filled by another prisoner. His model village, in its cardboard box, sits on the pillow, waiting to be posted.

James almost writes to Rose about the escape, but he doesn't want to worry her, and anyway the letter would pass through a German censor who would, he knows, delete any reference to it.

~~~

AFTER THE escape attempt, James doesn't see the Kommandant again. He remains in his office, doesn't come out to stand on his little wooden porch during roll call for a week after the killings. And then, the week after that, the prisoners are informed that they are to move and become part of another camp, with another Kommandant already in place there. The Kommandant at their Oflag is to remain behind with a few of the guards until he has orders to transfer elsewhere.

The prisoners are told about the move at the last minute. They're given half an hour to grab their belongings and what food they have left from the Red Cross parcels and assemble in the yard to begin the march. They are not told how far away the next camp is, how long they will be walking.

James wraps his notebook with his redstart findings in the piece of canvas the men in his bunk-house have been using to remove the kettle from the stove, and puts this package at the bottom of his rucksack. On top of it he places the letters from Rose and his parents, the German bird guide, and Davis's box with his model village, and on top of that he puts the last of a meat roll, some biscuits, a few squares of chocolate. It is not enough food for more than one meal. He hopes they won't be on the road for days.

"It must mean the Jerries are on the run," says Harry, stuffing a paperback novel in each jacket pocket, so that his uniform bulges like a packhorse. "They're probably moving us deeper into the heart of the Fatherland. Here's hoping the new camp is bigger and not as barren."

But James doesn't think of this camp as barren. He will miss the river, and the tree where he stood to watch the redstarts, and the old stone wall where they used to nest, and even the dark ashy colour of the limestone buildings in the rain. The new camp could very well be worse than this one, have less in it, especially if Harry is right and the Germans are on the defensive.

They march out of the camp gates four abreast, with guards positioned at the front and rear of the long line of prisoners.

They walk all morning and then stop for half an hour while the guards come down the line with buckets of water and a ladle. It's hot out, the sun directly overhead, all the men sweating in their filthy uniforms.

James crams a few biscuits into his mouth while he's waiting for his ladleful of water. He offers one to Harry, who is standing beside him in the line, but Harry shakes his head.

"Too thirsty," he says. He lights a cigarette. "Lovely day for a walk, though, isn't it?"

"A walk, not a march," says the Gardener, on the other side of James. "My boots aren't up to this. They're falling apart." He holds up a foot to show James and Harry how the sole of his boot has come away from the leather uppers and flaps open like a duck's bill.

They keep on for another few hours. James has blisters on both heels, making every step painful. He tries to forget about his feet, about the walk, about his body, and thinks instead about the redstarts, the ease and lightness of their flight above the river. He wonders where they are now, if any of the chicks survived into adulthood. And he wonders—absurdly, he knows—if any of the redstarts will remember him and miss his devoted vigil at the river.

The men start around a long curve in the road, deep woods on either side of them.

Harry leans over and whispers to James, "I'm going."

"What?"

"When we get to the middle of the curve, the guards will have either gone around it or not reached it yet. They'll be out of sight. I can just step off the road and into the woods. They won't notice I'm gone until you get to the new camp. I'll have hours on them."

"But you've always thought the tunnels stupid! You've only ever stayed in your bunk, reading. You don't want to escape."

"I've just been biding my time," says Harry. "Tunnels are a waste of energy, but this—this is an opportunity." He puts a hand on his friend's arm. "Be a sport and move over a bit after I'm gone so they don't notice the hole in the line."

"Harry." James doesn't know what to say. Harry Stevens has been his closest friend in the camp. He was counting on them seeing out the war together. What will he do without Harry in the bunk below, reading his novels and making snide remarks? Harry, always cheerful, making James feel better simply by virtue of his good nature. But James can't very well ask Harry to stay just because he will miss him. He can't ask him to stay just because James does not want him to go.

"I didn't know you at all," he says.

"You knew me," says Harry. He grins at James. "You just weren't an expert on me."

The guards at the front of the line are almost out of sight. James lowers the rucksack from his shoulders, takes out the remainder of his meat roll, and passes it to his friend.

"Think of me sometimes," he says. "And please, Harry, don't get yourself shot."

The front guards disappear around the bend.

Harry tucks the meat roll inside his shirt. "Bless you, James," he says, and he leans over and kisses him on the cheek. Then he steps down into the trees bordering the road, and he's gone.

Ash

——

Rose flicks on the reading lamp by her chair and turns over her husband's unopened letter in her lap.

Every week or two, she receives a letter from the camp where he is being held prisoner. Mostly he talks about the birds he is spotting around the area, or he asks her to look something up for him. He never mentions what is happening in the camp, or describes his surroundings, or even mentions the bloody weather. Each letter is simply a catalogue of bird behaviour, most of it so subtle and particular that Rose can't bring herself to care at all.

The dog raises her head, grunts, and flops back down on her blanket by the fire. Rose slides out of her armchair and onto the floor, putting her head on the dog's side, listening to Harris's heartbeat, loping fast and strong under her vaulted rib cage. The dog smells like wet socks and rotten fish. She must have rolled in something earlier that day.

The small cottage parlour looks cosy in the glow from the reading lamp. There are curtains at the window, a thick rug on the floor, chairs, a bookcase by the doorway with books and photographs on it. It is a modest home for a young married couple with prospects. They have rented this cottage from a friend of Rose's father who has charged them very little; the plan was to stay here until they started having children, and then they would need to look for something a little bigger.

The cottage is right on the lip of the Ashdown Forest and was once lived in by a shepherd. Until Rose and James moved in, peat—cut from a low boggy place on the forest and dried through the summer—was burned in the fireplace. The parlour still smells smoky and rich from the peat, the odour of it soaked right into the walls of the cottage.

At the back of the house is a large kitchen with a cooker and table, and a door that leads to the rear garden, much of which is taken up now with the chicken coop and Rose's Victory Garden. Upstairs there are two bedrooms tucked under the eaves and a water closet and bath, each in a separate tiny room, both of which must have been, in the shepherd's day, box cupboards.

Rose grew up near the Ashdown Forest, and although she went to London to work in an office for a year, she was happy to return to her childhood land-scape as a young married woman. She had found the grit and busyness of London unsettling. The quick-ness of life there always made her feel out of step, and her memories of that time all involve hurrying or being late.

Rose and James met in London. He was living there while doing his teacher training, and they had both joined a club called the Coffeepot to try to extend their meagre social lives. What Rose liked about James from the moment she met him was his quiet steadiness. In the midst of all the rush and bother of her London life, he felt like a place where she could shelter. For their first date they took a packed lunch to Hampstead Heath and looked for birds. Rose can't remember the birds they saw that day, but she does remember that they ate hard-boiled eggs and tomato sandwiches, and that the flask of tea they'd brought along was cold by the time they got around to drinking it.

The war has, of course, altered their plans for married life. Now Rose is here in the cottage by herself. She has chickens and a Victory Garden, her war job, Harris. She got the dog from a farmer near Duddleswell, on the other side of the forest. Since she was alone and fairly isolated in the cottage, it felt sensible to her to get a dog for companionship and protection. And Harris has not been a disappointment. No, the dog is not a disappointment.

Rose buries her face in Harris's neck, not caring that this is where the dead animal smell is the strongest.

AT TEN o'clock, Rose sets off on her appointed rounds. Later than usual, but not feeling very apologetic about it, she marches down the lane towards the road, Harris trotting optimistically behind her. In her rush to get out the door, Rose has forgotten her helmet and armband.

The edge of the forest is black, like a dark sea, but Rose knows the landscape so well that she never needs a torch to make her way down the lane from Sycamore Cottage.

The Bennetts have their blackout in place. So too does the house next to theirs, and the house next to that.

She knocks on the door of number forty-seven.

"There's some light showing on the second floor," she says when Mrs. Turner answers the knock. "Bedroom on the right. The curtains aren't quite pulled together."

"Thank you, Rose. I'll see to it. Goodnight now."

"Goodnight."

Rose continues down the road, knocking on two more doors to warn the occupants that their blackout precautions are inadequate.

When she gets to Mrs. Stuart's house it is as though she's standing in front of a bonfire. All the lights are blazing in the sitting room and bedrooms. None of the curtains are drawn.

"Again," she says to Harris, unlatching the gate and walking up the path to the front door.

Harris waits in the road, sniffing at the patch of ground where the rubbish bins usually stand.

Mrs. Stuart is close to sixty. She lost her husband in the first war and has been living alone since then. Her children never visit. Rose knows this because every night she has knocked on Mrs. Stuart's door to tell her to mind the blackout restrictions, and every night Mrs. Stuart has asked her to come in and help her with something, blaming her non-visiting children for the fact that she can't lift the coal scuttle or fix the door of the pantry. Most nights Rose has been obliging, has gone in, but tonight, she tells herself as she marches up the mossy stone path, she will not. It is late enough that surely Mrs. Stuart is thinking about retiring for the night.

Mrs. Stuart answers the door on the first knock, as though she was waiting right behind it, spying on Rose through the little window above the letterbox. She is wearing a red dressing gown. Her white hair is down and brushed to her shoulders.

"Rose, dear," she says, opening the door wider, "could you come in and help me with the pilot light in the cooker? It's gone out and I just can't reach that far in with the match."

"It's late," says Rose. "I really should be getting on. I still have half my sector to do."

"Oh, it won't take any time at all," says Mrs. Stuart. "How will I make do without the oven?"

"And I have the dog with me."

"I love the dog!" Mrs. Stuart claps her hands and shouts, quite loudly, into the front garden. "Harris! Harris! Come here, girl."

Harris bounds cheerfully up the path.

"Traitor," murmurs Rose under her breath as Harris shoots by, rushing down the carpeted hallway towards the kitchen. Mrs. Stuart often leaves a plate of scraps on the floor by the back door for her.

The kitchen is warm and stuffy, as though the windows haven't been opened in years. Rose kneels on the floor, her head angled into the oven. The interior smells burnt. The pilot light catches on the third match. When she pulls her head back out of the cooker, Mrs. Stuart hands her a cup and saucer.

"I thought you'd appreciate a nice cup of tea after your hard work, dear," she says.

"I really have to go, Mrs. Stuart."

Rose perches on the hard edge of a flowered wing chair in the sitting room, the cup and saucer balanced on her lap so she won't forget to drink the tea, and to drink it quickly.

The surfaces of the room are cluttered with memorabilia of the former Mr. Stuart—his medals, set in blue velvet and hung in a frame over the mantelpiece; numerous photographs of him in his officer's battledress. Rose has been given the tour of these artifacts so often that she knows their history as well as Mrs. Stuart does. But the one item she returns to voluntarily is the photograph of the Stuarts on their wedding day. In the photograph they are emerging from the arch of the church door into sunlight. Mrs. Stuart wears a white satin dress with a veil and a train; the veil is lifted back over her dark hair. Mr. Stuart is in his uniform. They walk through a corridor of swords raised by Mr. Stuart's fellow soldiers.

Rose likes to look at this photograph because the expression on Mrs. Stuart's face is one of such happiness that it always makes Rose happy to see it. But she can't seem to match the expression in the photograph with Mrs. Stuart's face now, although she tries every time she is at the house.

Harris saunters into the sitting room and comes over to Rose. She has gravy on her whiskers and her breath smells of rubbish.

"Mrs. Thomas, the one whose son was shot down

over the Channel last month," says Mrs. Stuart. "She's had word this morning that he's been captured." She sips at her tea delicately, clearly intending to make her cup last for at least an hour. "Perhaps he'll be taken to the same camp as James. Wouldn't that be nice?"

"I suppose so." Rose drains her tea in one gulp and burns the back of her throat.

"How is James? Have you had a letter?"

Rose thinks of the unopened letter on the table by her armchair and immediately feels guilty. She stands up, walks over to the sitting-room window, and decisively draws the curtains.

"I really have to be going, Mrs. Stuart. I still have two streets to cover, and I want to finish before midnight. It doesn't seem fair to wake people from their beds for the blackout."

"No, no. Of course not." Mrs. Stuart reluctantly puts her cup of tea aside. Before they're out of the sitting room, Harris has walked over and lapped up the rest of it.

"You're horrible," says Rose when they're outdoors. But she reaches down and rubs the top of the dog's head anyway.

~

THE NEXT morning Rose wakes up to the barking of a dog. At first she's confused because Harris lies sprawled across the end of her bed. But the barking continues, and when Harris, also waking to the sound, suddenly lifts her head and leaps off the eiderdown, Rose knows what's happening.

Clementine is sitting by the front door when Rose opens it. She bounds into the cottage, and she and Harris start wrestling in the hallway until Rose pushes them outside. The dogs race around the garden for a few revolutions and then head up onto the forest, running at top speed over the golf course greens and into the bracken beyond.

When Rose bought Harris, the farmer decided to keep one of the puppies himself. When the dogs were very young, Rose would take Harris over the forest to play with her sister. Now that the dogs are well over a year, they do the visiting on their own. Sometimes Rose will wake up to find Clementine downstairs, and sometimes she will wake up to find Harris gone.

Rose gets dressed and makes a cup of tea. The dogs return for breakfast, panting and muddy, their coats stuck with burrs.

Rose takes a slab of horsemeat from the larder

and slaps it onto two plates, putting one at one end of the kitchen and one at the other. If the dogs eat too close to each other, they fight over the food. They are best friends outdoors, but sometimes they scrap indoors.

It's a damp and misty morning. Rose finishes her tea, makes some toast, and scrapes butter across it from the end of her week's ration, adding a dollop of marmalade. Then she goes out to the hens to feed them and collect the eggs—eight this morning. She still hasn't used the seven from yesterday, so she'll package up a dozen and take them over to her parents today.

Rose stands at the back door eating another piece of toast and marmalade while the dogs sniff eagerly along the tracks of a rabbit. Rose hardly ever sits down for meals now. Her habits have grown slovenly in this new single life she has been forced to lead. She often sleeps on the floor with the dog in the sitting room. She eats standing at the open back door or bent over the sink. The abandonment of routine is a response to loneliness, she thinks. But it is also far less unpleasant than one would think to live in this new unstructured way.

Clementine is still inside when Rose is ready to set off on the journey across the forest to her parents' house. The dogs are lying together by the empty fire, sleeping off their breakfast. Harris has her head nestled into Clementine's neck. Two white dogs with the musculature of horses. English pointers. Almost identical.

"Walk," says Rose, and they scramble to their feet and get to the door before she does.

Rose has lived within sight of the Ashdown Forest most of her life. She knows the sight and feel of it, the smell of it, so well that she could probably find her way across it in the dark. Once a hunting park for Henry VIII, it has always been used by the inhabitants of the village as a necessary and sustaining feature of their daily lives. The bracken is still cut for animal bedding for those cottages and small farms on the outskirts that have cows and sheep. The spring in the centre field was once used as the water source for the villagers. Before it was a golf course, people hunted its copses and woods, shot birds from the open stretches of grass. Although it's called the Ashdown Forest, there are actually no ash trees on it. In fact, there are hardly any trees at all, because

Henry VIII cut them all down to build his navy. But there never were any ash trees. The land was named after a Frenchman who used to own it. The English couldn't pronounce his name, and the bastardized version became *Ash*.

Rose never gets tired of being out on the forest, of the smoky smell of the bracken and the mist sheathing the hollows. She likes the quiet of it, and how she can strike across it for a whole day and not meet a single person.

The dogs charge ahead of her. One of them has a stick and the other gives chase. They crash through the ferns and bushes with reckless exuberance. Rose sometimes feels she should have tighter control over them, but she also rather likes their joyful plunge through the morning.

The mist dissipates on the walk across the heath. The sun moves higher into the sky, and it slants across the bracken, warming Rose's face and releasing the smell of the earth—a rich, loamy perfume that is pleasant to breathe in and suddenly makes Rose feel hungry.

~~~

Rose doesn't knock at the front door of her parents' house but instead heads round the back. Her father is raking grass cuttings in the garden.

"Hello, Daddy." Rose puts the basket down and gives him a kiss on the cheek. Harris romps across the grass, barking her greeting. She's alone. Clementine left them at the top of the road, trotting happily home, no doubt to scrounge a second breakfast.

"Hello, darling. What a nice surprise."

"I've brought you some eggs."

"Lovely."

The back door of the house opens and Rose's mother, Constance, leans her head out and calls up the garden, "Rose, what are you doing? Come into the house at once."

"Be right there," Rose calls back. She turns to her father. "How are you, Daddy?"

Frederick sighs, then fumbles in his jacket pocket for a cigarette. "She's been blowing a regular gale, my darling," he says. He strikes a match, breathes the smoke deeply into his lungs. "I've been out here since daybreak. But it's no shelter."

"Rose!" calls Constance from the doorway.

"Nothing for it, then," says Rose. She picks up her basket. "Are you coming?"

"I'll stay and finish my smoke first, if you don't mind," her father says. "You know how she loathes the smell of it in the house."

"I'll leave Harris with you, then."

"That would probably be best."

Her mother holds the door open and ushers Rose inside. "Why don't you come to the front door, like a normal person?"

"I have the dog with me." Rose proffers the basket. "I brought you some eggs. The hens have been laying well this week."

Constance takes the basket. "Grubby little creatures. You don't still have that one in the house with you, I hope."

"Beatrice? No, she's healed up now and is back outside."

"You shouldn't name them, Rose."

They walk down the hallway towards the kitchen. "Why not?"

Constance opens the larder and puts the egg basket inside.

"Because they'll end up in a pot sooner or later,"

she says, slamming the door shut. "And it's harder to eat something that has a name."

"But I'm not going to eat them."

"Rose. You know nothing about war." Constance takes the lid off the tea tin and puts the kettle on the hob. "You'll stay for a cup of tea."

It's not a question, so Rose doesn't bother to answer. She watches her mother prepare the tea—warming the pot before the water boils, measuring the length of time the tea brews. Constance still wears her nurse's watch pinned to her blouse, even though she hasn't been a nurse since the end of the first war. But that watch comes in startlingly handy on a regular basis in Constance's daily life.

Frederick never returns to the house. Rose and her mother sit in the parlour to drink their tea. The carriage clock ticks loudly on the mantle. The china cups clatter on the saucers.

"James is well, then?" asks Constance.

"Yes. I had a letter this morning." Rose doesn't mention that she hasn't opened it yet.

"I hope you're working hard at keeping up his morale."

"I suppose I am."

"It's your duty, Rose." Constance sips at her tea. From outside, Rose can hear Harris barking. The dog is most likely protesting the fact that she's not been allowed into the house.

"When William went to serve, I wrote to him every day."

William was Constance's first husband. He died, impossibly young, in the first war, in his second month of fighting. Constance was a widow at nineteen. It was after that, after William's death, that she became a nurse and met her second husband, Rose's father, while she was working on the ward. He was her patient, a handsome young soldier with a bullet wound in his shoulder.

Rose wants to say that her mother would have had to write to William for only two months, whereas she's been dutifully sending letters to her husband for over six months now, and it gets a bit wearing. "I'm writing to James," she says.

"And saying nothing negative, I hope," says Constance. "He does not need to know about your petty grievances while he's got so much on his plate."

James's last letter was a series of questions, all relating to the redstarts. Rose had answered every

one, even though it took her a full two days of thumbing through reference books.

"I don't think he's doing anything useful over
there," she says. "But I don't complain."

"I'm sure he's sparing you the worst in his letters."

Rose puts her empty cup down on the saucer, and
then places the cup and saucer on the coaster on the
mahogany table beside her chair. The coaster is one in
a series with pictures of English villages. This spring-
time village is Alfriston. She recognizes the coaster
from her childhood and suddenly feels defeated by the
memory. "I'm going to take some tea out to Daddy,"
she says.

"Take a mug," says her mother. "I don't want him
chipping one of the Spodes. You know how he is."

ON ROSE's return journey across the heath, the
clouds are low and hang in the tops of the trees.
Harris, obviously tired from the strenuous exer-
cise of the morning, trots close by Rose. She's glad
of the dog's company. The early morning mist, the
low clouds, and the visit to her parents have left her

feeling lonely. She used to associate this feeling primarily with missing James. Those two things were directly equated—James was away and Rose missed him, felt lonely because he was gone from her daily physical life. But now that the reality of James has itself grown dim, Rose realizes that the feeling of loneliness she is constantly caught in might have nothing to do with her husband's actual absence. The loneliness might just be a condition she's always had, and while it disappeared in the first rush and flush of marriage—Rose and James wanted to secure their union before the war came and so married after knowing each other for only a few exhilarating months—it has returned now that her initial passion for her husband has diminished.

When Rose gets back to the cottage she's tired and chilled from her walk over the fields, and although she knows she should open James's letter— her mother's comments have made her feel guilty about not opening it—she instead lies with the dog on the floor of the sitting room and reads a book.

She wakes up two hours later, the book tipped off her chest and pointing towards the floor like a boat going under the waves. The wind rattles the glass panes at the front of the parlour. Rose gets up, a little stiffly, and goes into the kitchen.

She makes some toast and potted meat, then stands at the open back door, looking out at the tangle of greenery in her vegetable garden, and beyond that to the wood and wire of the chicken coop.

Rose doesn't open James's letter that evening. She finishes her book, feeds the chickens, has a bath. In the hallway, searching for her helmet and armband before she heads out on patrol, she catches a glimpse of herself in the mirror near the coats. There's no light on and her face is a smudge of darkness, but her eyes are as bright as a fox's.

THE NEXT morning when Rose wakes up, Harris is gone. She's not sure how long the dog will be off with Clementine, but Rose recognizes the moment as an opportunity. She washes and dresses, doesn't bother with breakfast, scatters some feed for the hens on her way out, and walks so quickly down to the village that the stones on the road chatter under her shoes the whole way.

It's breakfast at the Three Bells, so Rose doesn't need to have Toby rung for—he's simply there, eating toast and marmalade in the bar. He looks up when she approaches his table, his face breaking into a smile.

"I missed you yesterday."

"I had to go and see my parents." Rose sits down at the table.

"Are you hungry? Would you like some breakfast?" Toby reaches across and squeezes her hand, but Rose quickly pulls it back into her lap.

"I know everyone in this village," she says. "Or rather, everyone knows me." She looks around the bar, but there are very few people in the room and no one she recognizes among the small scattering of patrons. "Come to the cottage tonight. I'll make you supper."

"Are you sure?" Rose hasn't wanted Toby at the cottage before. The thought of it made her feel too guilty.

"Yes, I'm sure. Six o'clock." Rose stands up to go. "You'll probably get an omelette, I'm afraid. I have a lot of eggs to get through."

"I love a good omelette. I can't wait, my darling." Toby blows her a kiss from behind his napkin.

Rose walks slowly back up the road to her cottage. She's not sure it's a good idea to have Toby come to the house, but she can't keep sneaking into his room at the pub and expect to get away with it for much longer.

She wasn't looking for this kind of trouble. It just happened. And Rose can't seem to help herself. Best just to let the moments roll on, the momentum gaining acceleration with every touch or glance between them, so that by now what is to come feels inevitable and there is no stopping it.

Toby is stationed nearby, awaiting his orders to re-enter the war. Rose met him at the beginning of his leave, when he was wandering around on the forest, hopelessly lost, after taking himself there for a walk one afternoon. She helped him find his way. He invited her to tea. They laughed and talked well into the evening. He was easy to talk to, not like James, who was often quiet to the point of being withdrawn. Toby was cheerful and made Rose feel good. It felt natural to accept his kisses on the walk home. And now he is staying at the Three Bells so they can continue their affair on the room's single bed, with its lone pillow and scratchy pink eiderdown, the flash of swallows at the window, leaving and returning to their nest under the eaves.

When it started—when Rose first went upstairs with Toby through the servants' entrance, when she fell onto the bed with him and they fumbled the clothes from each other—she never once thought of James. And what she regrets now is not that she broke her marriage vows—a marriage so hastily made and of which so much came to be required—but that she could completely forget it in one swift flight of decisive action. She regrets that her marriage has come to mean nothing, has been worn down by the succession of days James has been away. She can no longer even imagine him, and the letters he sends, full of requests for her to do research for him, bring nothing useful to her, don't help to strengthen what has grown slack between them.

When Rose gets back to her cottage, Harris is waiting by the door, her coat streaked with mud. She seems subdued, and it takes Rose a minute to realize that the dog probably hasn't had any breakfast and is hungry.

"Sorry," she says, and unlocks the door. She gives Harris an extra-large helping of horsemeat, puts the kettle on to make herself some tea, and then forgets about it when it comes to the boil. She wanders into the parlour and then wanders back to the kitchen, not sure why she left it in the first place. She takes an apple out of the larder and leaves it on the table.

Harris finishes her breakfast and then goes to lie down on her blanket in the parlour.

Rose, never much of a cook, wants to make Toby something special tonight, something other than the omelette she promised. She still has her ration of meat to purchase this week. If the butcher has a bit of steak, maybe she can bake Toby a steak and kidney pie. She should be able to manage that. She spends some time thumbing through her one cookbook, and then some time blaming her mother for not teaching her how to cook properly. When she had asked her mother for some lessons once, Constance told her to work it out for herself. "I'm not much interested in cooking," she had said. Constance was always rail thin, and always finding everyone else too fat. "Gluttony is the worst of the sins," she said to Rose when she was young. "Mind you don't let yourself go."

"That's no help at all, is it?" says Rose to Harris. She has wandered back into the parlour. Harris, asleep on her blanket, offers no response.

Toby is prompt, arriving at Rose's front door at precisely six o'clock that evening. He is taller than James and has to duck his head under the door frame when he enters.

Harris, who had been sleeping up to the moment when Toby knocked at the door, bounds out of the parlour and jumps on him. The dog's enthusiasm makes Rose feel shy, as though Harris's excitement at seeing Toby is an embodiment of her own.

"Sorry," she says, hauling the dog off by her collar. "I don't get many visitors. She's really horribly behaved."

"Don't apologize," says Toby. "I like the candour of dogs. They're always honest about what they're feeling."

Rose, holding the powerful dog engine that continues to move forward, even while Rose is using all her strength to prevent this, realizes that the enthusiasm of Harris is also the embodiment of how Toby Halliday feels.

The cottage seems inadequate—poor and poky and full of dust. The biscuits she baked that morning to accompany their tea taste dry and bitter. The beef stew is cold. They sit either side of the small kitchen table, eating the stew and drinking the ale Toby brought from the pub.

"I'm sorry," says Rose. "I took the stew out sooner than I ought."

"It tastes delicious."

"And I left the biscuits in longer than I meant to."

"They're the best I've ever had."

"You washed each bite down with tea. I've been watching you."

Toby leans across the table and puts a hand against Rose's cheek. "Honestly, Rose. I've never had a better meal. More beautiful surroundings. More lovely company."

"You're a liar," says Rose, but she smiles and kisses his hand where it lies against her face.

She had feared that it would be too hard to have Toby Halliday at the cottage, but it isn't. It feels like he has always been there with her, and James seems as distant as the shepherd whose house the cottage used to be. Rose can't conjure him up at all, although she's also not trying very hard.

"I love you," she says.

"I love you too."

Upstairs in her double bed under the sloping ceilings, with the curtains drawn against the half darkness, Rose and Toby lie on their backs, holding hands and talking. This is so different from being with James, who was furtive when making love to Rose, coupling only when the lights were out, awkwardly flailing on top of her like a fish hauled from the ocean and left to die on shore. Afterwards he always curled into himself, not talking, falling asleep immediately.

"Will you stay?" asks Rose. "Here. For the whole night?"

"On one condition." Toby squeezes her hand. "That come morning, you make me that omelette you promised."

"It would be my pleasure."

Having Toby in the cottage hasn't erased James so much as replaced him with a better version. Rose married the wrong man. It is that heartbreakingly simple. And what is she going to do about it now?

In the next morning's post is a letter. Rose's heart sinks. She hasn't even read the last letter from James yet. But when she plucks the envelope from the metal cage at the front door, she doesn't recognize the return address, printed neatly in blue ink in the top left corner of the envelope. This letter is not from the German prison camp but from London.

It's a letter from James's sister, Enid, who wants to come and stay with Rose. She's been bombed out of her flat and left homeless.

I know you have the room, she writes, rather rudely. *And I have nowhere else to turn.*

Rose has met Enid only once, when she came to the wedding. She remembers her as sharp-tongued— James's elder sister and still bossing him around as though they were children. She'd given them binoculars as a wedding gift, which had rather pleased James but had disappointed Rose. She would have preferred wine glasses to spyglasses.

"I don't want her here," she whispers to Harris, who has wandered into the hallway to see what's up. Toby is finishing his breakfast in the kitchen. "Why can't she go and stay with her parents?" But Rose knows the answer to that question the moment she asks it. James's parents live in a small flat in Bristol. James's father had a stroke at the beginning of the war, and they had to move from their farm. There would be no room for Enid there, and it's a lot farther from London, which presumably she'll be returning to before very long.

Rose stands in the hallway, holding the letter from Enid. She can hear Toby running the water to wash the breakfast dishes, another thing James never did once in their brief life together.

She can't very well refuse James's sister the shelter she requests. But having Enid to stay will mean that Toby will be banished to the Three Bells once more, and that Rose will not be able to step into the new life she wants so badly. Instead, she will have to step back into a marriage that no longer feels like it belongs to her.

Rabbit

————

ENID DECIDES TO GET OFF THE TRAIN IN EAST Grinstead and walk the three-mile hill down into Forest Row. She has only one small suitcase and it doesn't weigh much, filled as it is with the few pieces of clothing she has managed to salvage from her bombed flat.

It's a pleasant day, the sun stirring from behind the clouds for a change, the air not too cool. No breeze.

The hill curves down from the town into the village. The suitcase bangs against Enid's legs as she walks, and for a good part of the journey she carries it in her arms instead of holding it by the handle. Trees crowd the edge of the road, and behind them, down long driveways, Enid can glimpse the large houses of the richer Sussex residents. Money buys privacy, she thinks, rather scornfully. Money makes it possible to live behind the screen of yews, behind the stone wall, and go about your business as usual. Money makes it possible to forget about the war—especially here, where there aren't bombs falling every night and heaps of debris to negotiate every day.

The last time Enid was in this part of England was for James's wedding. She was surprised that he'd decided to marry someone he'd known for only a few months. She'd assumed the thoroughness— almost caution—that had been on display since childhood would hold true in all circumstances, even love. But the war had no doubt helped to speed the romance along.

And now her brother was a prisoner somewhere in Germany, and here she was, on her way to live, temporarily, with his young wife. Enid was glad that James was in relative safety in the POW camp instead of still being in active service. He would be a terrible soldier. She'd told him this when he joined up. "You can't even kill an ant," she had said. "What will you do when you have to kill a person?"

But James had circumnavigated that problem by signing up for the air force, so, as he explained to his sister, he wouldn't actually have to see the people he was killing.

Thank god he'd been captured before he'd dropped even a single bomb.

Enid regrets getting off the train early. She thought it would be a way to ease into her new situation, the slow walk down the hill giving her time to adjust to being in the country and having to come and live with Rose. But instead, her suitcase is awkward and hard to manage, and the houses of the wealthy Sussex inhabitants are irritating her. She also doesn't like how the trees mass so densely at the side of the road. They don't soften her mind towards the pastoral, but instead make her feel jumpy and claustrophobic. There was more breathing room in London, even with the bombs falling.

But thinking about London brings back the sights and sounds of that terrible night two weeks ago, and Enid has to dodge that memory as much as possible if she is to keep functioning today.

The village bores her. A posh country hotel, a village hall, a parade of shops, a memorial to the local lads who perished in the first war. Nothing distinctive. No pond or close-clipped green. The pub looks cosy, but there's no one to have a drink with here, so she walks quickly past the Three Bells and on up Ashdown Road.

When she gets close to the row of cottages at the top of the road, she stops for a moment, sniffing the air like a dog. The burning smell is familiar, but it's a smell from far back in her life, from the days of her childhood, at the farm with her parents and James. It takes her several minutes to place it. Peat. It's the smell of burning peat. A rich, dense, dark smell, almost like pipe tobacco, that conjures up the smoky farmhouse kitchen in Dorset.

Enid prides herself on her memory and good navigation skills. Quite frankly, she would have made a better soldier than James. Despite having been to her brother's rented cottage only once before, she is able to pick it out immediately. The small stone building looks rough enough to have once been a stable, more fit for animals than humans.

The gate creaks. The path is overgrown with weeds. No one answers her knock at the front door. Enid tries again, harder this time, banging with her closed fist on the thick wooden slab, the action making her suddenly feel like crying.

No one comes to answer the door. Enid stops knocking. She goes round to the back of the cottage, getting scratched in the process by a scraggly climbing rose at the side of the house.

There's a chicken coop in the far corner of the garden and an overgrown vegetable patch closer to the cottage. There's also a dog, sitting patiently on the flagstones outside the kitchen door.

"Hello there," says Enid. She didn't know that Rose and James had a dog. She puts out a hand for the dog to sniff, but the dog remains steadfast in its task of staring fixedly at the closed door.

There's no answer at the back door either. Enid puts her suitcase on the flagstones and sits on it. She's tired from her walk down the hill, and she could do with a cup of tea and a sandwich. She's had nothing to eat all morning. How rude of Rose to be purposefully out when she arrives. Surely she received her letter with the time of the train?

This is not what Enid wants at this moment, to have nothing to occupy her mind but the night she is trying so hard not to think about. She supposes she could take a tour of the garden, visit the hens, try to identify the various flowers that have withered to stalks in the beds. But that would be so tedious. She scuffs the heel of her shoe across the stones. Her shoes are worn down from the London pavements and won't last the summer. For a moment she lets herself remember crawling over wood and plaster in what had once been the sitting room of her flat. There was a shoe upright in the midst of the debris, as though the foot had just stepped out of it.

"There you are!" It's Rose, marching across the garden with another dog at her heels, identical to the one sitting vigil at the back door.

Enid stands up. "Yes, here I am. Didn't you get my letter?"

"Of course I got your letter." Rose is flustered, her face red. She must have walked quickly up the rise of Ashdown Road. "I went to meet your train."

"But I didn't ask you to meet my train."

"I thought it would be nice."

"I got out early. Walked down from East Grinstead."

"Well, how was I to know that?"

"How was I to know you'd meet my train?"

This is the most they've ever spoken. Enid remembers Rose as shy and serious. Now she seems snappy and churlish. Still, James's absence must be hard on her. Enid puts out a hand. "Thank you," she says. "For taking me in. I'm sure it's an inconvenience, and I appreciate it."

"Glad to help," says Rose, not sounding glad at all. She doesn't shake Enid's outstretched hand.

The dogs are wrestling in the dusty bit of ground in front of the chicken coop.

Rose unlocks the door. "Are you hungry?"

"Famished."

"Well, come in, then. I'll make us some lunch."

Enid follows Rose into the kitchen. The house is as she remembers, dark and low ceilinged. This confirms her earlier thought that it was once a stable. It's easy to picture straw on the stone floor and a cow or a couple of sheep standing contentedly about, masticating.

"James never mentioned a dog in his letters," she says, watching the dogs through the small window as they tear around the garden. "Let alone two."

"They're sisters. Only one is mine. Harris. The other one, Clementine, lives across the forest. They like to visit each other." Rose turns from the pantry. "I could make you eggs and toast?" she says.

"Lovely. Thank you."

"I got the dog after James was taken prisoner. For company."

"Well, I'm sure that James will like him. There was always a dog on the farm when we were growing up."

"Her," says Rose. "The dog is a bitch. Harris. I call her that because it sounds like the name one would call an assistant. A last name instead of a first. She is my assistant. My companion." She breaks two eggs into a bowl. "Why don't you take your case upstairs while I'm making lunch? Yours is the first room at the top of the landing. I'm afraid it's a bit cramped. It was meant to be the nursery."

The ceilings are even worse upstairs than down. They slope at alarming, skull-cracking angles, and Enid anticipates knocking herself cold just getting out of bed in the night to go for a wee. The small room she has been given looks down into the back garden. She has a perfect view of the chicken coop and the back hedge. In London, she looked down onto the tops of buses, onto people walking briskly along Union Street on their way to work and then home again. In London, she was part of the shifting human landscape of the city. Here there is nothing but vegetation and a few brainless hens.

But when she goes back downstairs, the toast and scrambled eggs taste better than she expected. The tea is good and hot. They eat at the little table in the kitchen with the back door open so the dogs can come and go as they please. The breeze from the garden is warm and fragrant with the scent of flowers, something Enid realizes has been absent from her life these past months. London smells of plaster dust and burnt wood and the sharp, caustic aroma of cordite.

"I'm sorry if I was rude," says Rose. "Earlier. When you arrived."

I know when you mean, you idiot, thinks Enid, but she doesn't say this. "No need to apologize," she says instead. "It's not an ideal situation, my having to come down here and bunk with you. I'm sorry to intrude. Really, I am. But rest assured, I'll be gone as soon as I can find another job."

"You lost your job *and* your flat?"

"Yes. It wasn't a very good week." Understatement, Enid thinks. It was the worst week of her life.

Rose rises to fetch the dogs their dinner, as they've both suddenly materialized in the kitchen, humid and panting. "What did you do in London?"

"What was my job, you mean?"

"Yes."

Enid watches Rose slap down great chunks of horsemeat onto two plates and put them on the floor for the dogs. The meat is gulped down almost before the plates hit the stone tiles.

"I worked for an advertising agency," she says. "I was the assistant to one of the owners of the firm."

"Has the war affected advertising?" asks Rose.

Enid can see where she's headed. "I didn't lose my job because of the war," she says, standing up and pushing her chair neatly into the table, just as she was taught at boarding school when she was six, and as she has continued to do at every meal since, the surprising legacy of an institution she loathed.

"Thank you for lunch. It was lovely. And now, if you'll excuse me, I think I would like to go upstairs and unpack."

~~~

ENID SITS on the bed beside her suitcase. It makes no sense to unpack. It will seem as though she has more possessions if she leaves them in the case, rather than spreading them sparsely through the bureau on the wall opposite. She wishes she'd been able to rescue something other than clothing from the blast. A book, perhaps, or a flower vase. Even a ruddy fork.

The thoughts of that night are pushing into her head against her will. She goes over to the window to see if the dogs are up to anything interesting, but there's no sign of them in the garden. They're no doubt sleeping off their great hunks of horsemeat. Enid supposes she could go and try to engage with Rose again, hard work as it's been so far. She could go and look around the house, at any rate. That might work to keep her mind at rest.

There's an airing cupboard on the upstairs landing, and the closed door of Rose's bedroom across the hall. Enid wants to have a look inside that room but fears the door will squeak on its hinges, so she leaves it shut.

Downstairs there's a pitifully small parlour. Enid sits in a chair by the bookcase. It's lumpy and uncomfortable, overstuffed. The sun at the low window is not even enough light to enable her to read the spines of the volumes beside her. She wishes that she didn't find knitting so slappingly dull, or that she was interested in drawing. How on earth is she going to pass the weeks she'll be forced to spend in this dreadful little hovel without going batty?

Rose pokes her head into the room. "I'm off to the shops, then."

"Here's my ration book." Enid fumbles it out of her cardigan pocket, hands it over. "Could I make a request for some meat? A bit of beef, perhaps? Maybe a chop?"

"I'll see what I can manage." Rose pops her head out of the room and then pops it back in again. "If the dogs want out, just let them go."

"Will do. Do you want some money?"

"You can buy the next round."

Enid listens to the kitchen door snap shut. The dogs don't even lift their heads at the sound. She nudges the nearest dog with her foot, and it grunts and rolls over onto its back, exposing its hairless pink belly. Upside down it looks a bit like a pig. She waits a decent interval, long enough for Rose to be well down the road, and then she gets up and goes back upstairs.

The door to Rose's bedroom does indeed squeak on its hinges when Enid pushes it open. She steps inside. The room is at least three times the size of the one she has been given. It has two windows—one that looks down on the front garden, and a smaller one that overlooks the side of the cottage, where the scratchy rose grows up the stone. There are the same sloping ceilings that Enid has in her room and a larger version of her bureau. On top of the bureau are a silver-backed mirror and a clothes brush. On the bedside table is a photograph of James and Rose the day they were married. The curtains are flowery and pulled back. There is a wardrobe in the corner and a small Turkish carpet on the floor beside the bed. There is barely any evidence of Rose in her own bedroom, and the only indication of James, aside from his presence in the photograph, is the heavy wooden trouser press bulwarked up against the side of the wardrobe.

Enid stands by the bedside table and looks at her brother and his young wife on their wedding day. Ten years still seems like too large a gap in age and experience. When James married her, Rose was only twenty-two. Now she's just twenty-three. What can she possibly know about anything? Still, in the photograph, James looks happy, his smile wide and his eyes bright. He stands on the church steps in his best suit. Rose has hold of his right arm with both of her hands, as though she can't pull him in close enough to her that day. And Rose is beautiful. Even in the black and white of the photograph, her dark hair shines and her face is radiant.

In the weekly letters she writes to James at the camp, Enid never mentions Rose. She wouldn't know what to say about her. She tells her brother about London life, about what she sees on the streets or in the shop windows. She never mentions the bombings, or the scarcity of food either. She thinks it must help him to have positive news of home, to be able to imagine the flavour of the world that continues, as he remembers it, outside the cage where he is being kept. But Enid is not really sure her cheerful disregard for his circumstances is the right approach. That said, it is one he mirrors, sending her letters back that describe the birds he has seen around the camp. Sometimes he asks her to look something up about a particular bird, and she especially likes those letters because they make her feel useful.

She did write to James and tell him that she was coming down to stay with Rose in the cottage, and he did write back to say that he thought it was a wonderful idea, and that Rose would be glad of the company.

But Rose isn't glad of the company. Enid can clearly see that from their testy exchanges today. And yet, standing here in her sister-in-law's sparsely furnished bedroom, Enid wonders why Rose isn't pleased to have her come and stay. What kind of life can she be living, isolated in the countryside with only two dogs for companionship, and just the hens and the patchy garden as evidence that she is doing anything useful with her days?

There are still hours to go before tea time, and Enid is too restless to write to James or try to read a book. She doesn't want to be alone in the cottage with her uncomfortable thoughts, so she decides to go and explore the stretch of heath she can see from Rose's bedroom window.

The dogs shoot through the door ahead of her the moment she opens it. They are gone—blurred, muscled forms racing across the bracken. They run so hard and so fast that the way their paws come together and then push apart in the action of their running reminds Enid of the clench and unclench of a heart. The dogs' gathering in and pushing off happening in the steady rhythm of a heartbeat.

They're gone, just like that, and Enid walks out into a field of grass and rusted ferns, pink heather and mounds of yellow gorse. It is prettier than she'd thought. The summer sun looks lovely in its halo above the birches.

She walks and walks, filling her pockets with the small flowers and ferns she doesn't know the names of, walks until her mind is numb with fatigue. She sees a rabbit sitting upright in the bracken, ears cupping the sounds of her approach. Luckily the dogs aren't around to see it too, chase it down and pull it to pieces. Enid stops for a moment, watching the delicacy of its whiskers twitching in the watery sun, the stubble-coloured weft of its fur.

There was a rabbit in London the night her flat was bombed. She was standing outside the building, watching the firemen arc their hoses into the flames, destroying in the process what hadn't already been burned or crushed. She was standing with the other inhabitants of Union Street when she heard someone say, "Look, there's a rabbit!" And sure enough, at the base of a lamppost was a white rabbit. It must have been a pet, or perhaps kept for food, and its cage had been ruined in the blast. Now it was free in the centre of London, on a busy street where it was sure to get run over. How strange, Enid had thought at the time, that the safer place for an animal that had once been wild was in captivity. Standing there, her life finished, the ambulance with Oliver's body disappearing up the street, Enid had wanted nothing more than to save the rabbit, to catch it and keep it with her in a box until she could build it a cage. But the moment she stepped towards it, the rabbit hopped along the pavement, away from her and into shadow.

When Enid returns to the cottage, Rose still isn't back from the shops. It's past tea time and coming on to supper. The eggs that Enid had for lunch have worn off, and she's hungry again. It seems polite to wait for Rose, as Enid is a guest in her house, but after an hour, Enid thinks, Sod this, and ravenously starts poking through the larder, looking for something to eat. She finds a tin of salmon and boils a couple of potatoes to go with it. There's an opened bottle of red wine under the sink, probably for cooking, but she helps herself to a liberal glass of it anyway. After the third mouthful, it tastes just fine. While she is eating at the little table in the kitchen, Enid spreads out beside her plate the flora she has brought back from the Ashdown Forest. She is sure that James will have reference books in the cottage, and after she has eaten she will go to look up these wisps of grass and scraps of flower. It will be good to know what it is she's found. It will feel like she's accomplished something today.

Rose and Toby are lying naked on the single bed in his room at the Three Bells. The bed is so narrow that they are forced to lie on top of each other, and since this tends to lead to another round of lovemaking, they have been here hours longer than they intended.

Rose has seen the window shimmer with dusk and then close to darkness. She knows it is late, but she doesn't dare ask Toby the time, even though his watch ticks right against her ear. She is horribly worried and doesn't care at all, both feelings happening simultaneously. She can't remember being this much in love with James, but she must have been. Why would she have married him otherwise?

It's all so confusing, and mostly what Rose wants in this moment is simply to kiss Toby again, to brush her hand across his face, to nestle into the hollow between his neck and collarbone (for she is lying on top this time).

"I can't go," she says, "and yet I feel dreadful that Enid is waiting up at the cottage for me. I wasn't very nice to her today. And she is James's sister. It's not her fault that her flat was bombed."

"Who are you trying to convince?" asks Toby, running his hand over Rose's bare back.

"Myself, I guess."

"And to what purpose?"

"So that I'll like her more than I do. So that I won't feel so guilty about not liking her."

"Ah. Here's a question: Does it matter whether you like her or not?"

"No, I suppose not." Rose pushes up from his chest so that she can look into his blue eyes. "And truthfully, I don't really think she likes me much either."

"There you go, then. Mutual loathing. Nothing like it." Toby smiles and Rose thinks that he is much more handsome than James, and though she shouldn't care about something as petty as this, she enjoys making the comparison anyway.

Toby walks Rose home, up Ashdown Road in the dark, right to the edge of the path to her cottage. She won't let him come any farther in case Enid has retired upstairs and sees them in the back garden.

They stand at the edge of the path, kissing in the shadows of the trees, not wanting to break apart.

"I should go," says Toby.

"Yes," agrees Rose. "You should go." But this announcement just makes them cling more tightly together.

Something knocks into Rose and she squeals loudly enough for Toby to clamp a hand over her mouth. It's the dogs, back from their day on the forest, banging exuberantly against her legs. They are ecstatic at finding Rose in the darkness, so close to the cottage where the horsemeat is kept and where there is a warm blanket in the sitting room to lie on and rest their tired bones.

"They've got something," says Toby. The dogs

are tugging at opposite ends of what looks like a coat sleeve. He bends down, pries Harris's jaws open, and dangles the item in front of Rose. "Looks like they've caught a rabbit." The carcass of the animal hangs from his fingers; all that's left is the skin and the four paws.

"Horrid dogs," says Rose. "They're very good hunters, I'm afraid. Don't throw it away. They'll just go after it again."

Toby slings the rabbit skin over his shoulder, like a poacher. "I'll dispose of it on my way back to the pub," he says. "Better get those hellions indoors before they kill something else." He gives Rose a quick kiss and turns to make his way back down the road.

The dogs crowd against Rose, not minding that their prize has been taken away, glad to have found her instead. She pats their flanks, scratches the tops of their heads. "Come on, you horrible dogs," she says. "Let's go home."

Thankfully Enid is in bed when Rose gets in. There's nothing to eat, and she forgot to go to the shops, even though that had been her excuse for leaving the cottage. She breaks off a hunk of cheese from the block in the larder and eats it standing in the middle of the kitchen. I'm turning into an animal, she thinks, but the thought doesn't really displease her.

She leaves the dogs in the cottage when she goes back out a half hour later on patrol. It seems that Clementine means to stay the night. She has made no move to leave, and Rose doesn't bother trying to make her go. If she stays it means the dogs will remain downstairs and she won't have to share her bed with Harris.

It's dark and cold and she's tired. Love is exhausting, or perhaps it's the lack of food. In any case, she'd rather be home than marching through the streets of Forest Row, looking for slivers of light leaking from the darkened houses.

Mercifully, people are obedient tonight and there are only a few transgressors. But of course, when she gets to Mrs. Stuart's house the lights are all blazing and not a single curtain is drawn.

Rose sighs, opens the gate, walks up the path, bangs on the front door. No response. She bangs again. Usually Mrs. Stuart is waiting right behind the door, eager to entice Rose inside with some flimsy excuse for company. So it's strange that the old woman doesn't answer. Rose bangs on the door for a third time. Nothing. She jumps off the stoop and down into the front garden, treading on a flower bed so she can peer through the sitting-room window.

There, lying on her back on the carpet, one leg twisted under her at an odd angle, is Mrs. Stuart. She's wearing an apron. Her spectacles, which must have come off her face when she fell, are lying by the fire.

Rose raps on the window with her fist. She calls Mrs. Stuart's name. There's no response. She rushes round to the back garden and tries the kitchen door. It's locked. All the windows are shut fast.

No one answers next door when Rose knocks there. It's late. Everyone must be in bed by now; the whole street is dark and silent. She stands for an indecisive moment in the road, not knowing what to do. Her cottage isn't far. She can rush home, grab something to break a window, and come back to Mrs. Stuart's house, all within minutes. And she'll bring Enid with her for support. Enid's been through an emergency. She'll be helpful. She'll know what to do.

~~~~

ENID WAKES up to her name being called, often and urgently. She struggles upright and stumbles out to the top of the stairs. Rose is halfway up the staircase, still shouting for her.

"What is it?" Enid says, hurrying down. "What's the matter?"

"Mrs. Stuart's collapsed. I need you to help me break into her house."

Enid looks at her sister-in-law. "Why are you wearing a helmet?"

"I'm in the ARP. Why are you fully dressed?"

"It's very damp in your house, if you haven't noticed." Enid grabs Rose's arm and they hurry through the kitchen to the back door. "To stay warm, I went to sleep in all my clothes."

The dogs, woken by the excitement, try to follow them, but Rose slams the door before they can muscle through. She whips open the shed and grabs a shovel. As they rush past the chicken coop, she realizes, with a pang of guilt, that she's forgotten to feed the hens.

They hurtle down the road in the dark. It's only been ten minutes, maybe fifteen, since Rose left Mrs. Stuart's house, and nothing has changed. She rushes towards the sitting-room window. Mrs. Stuart still lies motionless on the carpet. Rose raises the shovel, but Enid puts a hand on her arm.

"No, don't. It will be expensive for her to fix. Here. Let me." She takes the shovel from Rose and, hopping nimbly onto the stoop, breaks the small window that flanks the door, then reaches in and turns the bolt. She opens the door for Rose.

In the sitting room it's Enid who's all business. She bends over Mrs. Stuart, lifting her wrist to feel for a pulse.

"Call an ambulance," she says to Rose. "There's a pulse. He's alive."

Rose finds the telephone in the hallway by the kitchen. When she returns to the sitting room, Enid is still crouched beside Mrs. Stuart, holding on to her wrist.

"They're on their way," says Rose.

Enid doesn't look up. "His pulse is too rapid," she says. "I think he may be in shock."

The ambulance comes. The men with their boots on seem huge and ungainly in Mrs. Stuart's fussy front room. They haul her onto a stretcher, and at the sudden movement, she comes to, starts groaning.

"What's the matter with her?" asks Rose.

The taller ambulance attendant shrugs his shoulders. "Stroke," he says. "Heart attack. You never know with the old dears. It could be anything. Their bodies are bombs, waiting to go off."

Mrs. Stuart is loaded into the ambulance. Enid goes over to talk to the attendants as Rose is turning out the lights in the house and drawing the curtains. When Rose comes back outside, the ambulance is gone and Enid is standing on the stoop, smoking a cigarette.

"We'll have to call someone," says Enid.

"She has children. I'll go and look for her handbag." Rose hesitates by the front door. "I didn't know you smoked," she says.

Enid exhales. "I stopped months ago. Cadged one off the ambulance driver. It felt like a good night to start up again."

"You were very professional in there," says Rose. "Thank you." She has her hand on the doorknob but takes it off again. "But why did you keep calling Mrs. Stuart a he?"

"I did that?" Enid draws on her cigarette, exhales. "I didn't know I was doing that."

She tries to concentrate on the smoke rising up into the darkness, on the glowing tip of her cigarette, but it's too late. Her mind is filling with images. There's the man's shoe, upright in the debris, a whole room away from where Oliver lies crushed under the ceiling beams.

"How is it possible," she says, "for a shoe to come off a foot and the laces still to be tied?"

"What?"

Enid leans against the door. "How is it possible?" she says again.

"Are you all right?" asks Rose.

"No, I don't think I am."

"Here, come and sit down."

Rose leads Enid to the edge of the stoop. They sit down, Enid leaning her body into Rose the way Harris sometimes does when there's a thunderstorm. When Enid starts to cry, Rose puts her arm around her. They sit like that for several minutes, not speaking. The night around them is silent, and they become absorbed into that silence.

Then an owl hoots from a nearby tree.

There's the slam of a door down the road. The clink of milk bottles being set out on a front step.

Enid wipes her eyes with her coat sleeve. "I had a lover," she says. "Oliver. He died in my flat the night it was bombed."

"Oh, god," says Rose.

"It gets worse. He was my boss. My married boss. No one knew of our affair, and when he died, it all became public. I had to leave my job, flee London. I'm a fugitive, Rose. I came here to hide out."

Rose squeezes Enid's shoulder. "You're safe with me," she says. "You can be a fugitive here as long as you like. The forest is a very good place to hide out. Look how well it shelters all the animals that live on it."

Enid laughs. "Am I an animal, then? A rabbit shivering in its burrow?"

"I think of you as something a little more predatory than that," says Rose, which makes Enid laugh again.

"SHE'S NO different from you, then," says Toby, when Rose tells him the story of Enid and her married lover.

"You're not married."

"But you are." Toby props himself up on his elbow. "Rose, what are we going to do about it?"

"I don't know."

They're lying on the floor of the sitting room in Rose's cottage. Enid has gone out for the day. She's taken a packed lunch and has said she won't be back until dark. The moment she left, Rose ran down to the Three Bells to fetch Toby. They've spent the morning in bed, and now they're downstairs, on the pretext of eating, but they haven't made it as far as the kitchen yet.

"What are you going to do about James?"

"Can't we just go on like this?" Rose asks. "It's not as though he's coming home any time soon."

"Yes, but I'll be going. And I want to go into the war with some reassurance that you're mine."

"I am yours."

"Not as long as you're married to another man."

It seems to Rose that this is how she was persuaded to marry James—the threat of his disappearance into the war. But the truth is that she feels more certain about her feelings for Toby than she did her feelings for James. And in this moment, it seems an easy thing to give Toby Halliday what he wants.

"I'll write to him," she says, "and ask for a divorce."

"Promise?"

"Yes."

"Because I'll never love anyone the way I love you, Rose. I want to marry you. I want to travel the world with you."

Toby is set to take over his father's tea-importing business when the war is over. He will work in a small office in London, and it is unlikely that they will be able to travel the world, but Rose doesn't say anything to dissuade him. She likes his passion for her, and she likes how that passion expands to include everything around him. They are evenly matched— the same age, the same excited feelings for each other. If Toby is willing to believe that they will have a life of adventure together, then Rose is willing to believe it too. She will go where he goes because she wants only to be with him, and it doesn't matter to her where they live.

They make love again. Then Rose goes into the kitchen to get Toby a cup of tea before he has to leave for the pub. The dogs, gone since breakfast, are at the back door when she puts the kettle on the hob. She lets them in and they bound into the cottage to greet Toby. When Rose comes back with the tea, he's wrestling with both dogs on the sitting room floor.

"Careful," she says. "They're demanding when they love you."

Toby has Harris in a headlock. She squirms free and he grabs her again. "I like dogs," he says. His face is red from the exertion of wrestling. He grins at Rose. He looks happy, she thinks, setting the tea tray down on the coal box. Today I have made one man happy, and tomorrow I will set about making another very unhappy.

Dragonfly

ENID IS UP ON THE HEATH BY NINE IN THE MORN-
ing with her specimen bag and her books. She has
been at this for several days now and has a system
worked out. Using a detailed map she found in one of
her brother's reference books, she focuses on a particular area of the forest one day, a different area the
next. She picks samples of flowers and ferns, writes
down in her notebook the names of any animals she
sees. At one o'clock she breaks for lunch, spreads
her mackintosh on the ground, and unwraps her
sandwiches or peels a hard-boiled egg. At two she is
back on task again. At four she is hurrying across the
heath, home to Sycamore Cottage.

These are roughly the hours she kept when she was working at the agency, and it is comforting to fall back into this routine, to lean on work, any work, as though it is something solid and will hold her up.

The minutiae of Ashdown Forest are more interesting than she first assumed. Each little flower has a history and cultural references, is a superstition or cure for something. Everything is its own world, and if Enid stays there, in these worlds, she won't have to break the surface of the large, terrifying world she actually lives in.

In the evenings, Enid spreads out her specimens on the kitchen table, and she identifies them with the help of her reference books. She's not sure what she will do with her account when it is finished, but she has a vague idea that she might send it to James in Germany. He would appreciate her attempt at writing a natural history. He might like to be so precisely reminded of home, to read about the grasses and the deer and the birds up on the forest and imagine himself there again.

"Don't tell me you're still at it," says Rose when she comes home that evening to find Enid thumbing through her wildflower guide.

"Come here," says Enid. She brandishes a stalk for Rose to see. "A heath spotted-orchid. Look at how perfect these tiny petals are."

Rose regards the tiny flower that Enid holds out to her. "Beautiful," she says.

"But you don't mean that." Enid retracts the orchid.

Rose puts her basket down on the worktop. "I was able to get a couple of chops," she says. "I'm going to make us a nice supper tonight."

"I'm not your damned dog," says Enid. "You can't coax me back to favour with food."

Rose laughs. "Can't I?"

"Well, you can't immediately coax me back."

Enid moves her natural history samples to one end of the table and sets out the cutlery and plates on the other.

"I made an apple crumble for pudding," says Rose.

"You have splashed out. What's the occasion?"

"No occasion. I'm just ..." Rose wants to say "happy," but she's worried that Enid will wonder how she can be happy when James is still being held prisoner. "Happy to do it."

"Well, I'm certainly happy to eat it."

Rose puts the chops in a pan under the grill.

"Shall we have a drink?" she asks. "There's a half-finished bottle of plonk under the sink."

"I'll do the honours." Enid takes down two glasses from the cupboard, pours the dregs of the red wine into the glasses, and hands one to Rose. "Here's looking up your old address," she says. They clink.

"I think candles would be nice," says Rose. She hurries into the sitting room and comes back with a pair of white candles in silver candlesticks. She puts them in the centre of the table, lighting the wicks with the box of matches she keeps on the back of the cooker. "They were a wedding present," she says. "I think we only ever used them once."

Rose remembers that supper. She had made a cauliflower cheese for James. It was one of the first times she had cooked for him, one of their first meals together as a married couple. She had thought the candles would be a nice touch, romantic, but James had complained that he couldn't see his food and blew them out. After that she put them on top of the book-case and never brought them out again.

"Very nice," says Enid. "Candles make a meal more festive, don't you think?"

"I do."

They eat the chops and mash and peas. Their forks click against the plates. There's the sound of the tap dripping into the sink.

Rose clears and brings the pudding.

"It's very good," says Enid.

"It's nice to have someone to cook for again," says Rose. "Did you cook much for yourself in London?"

"Mostly I ate in pubs. I often worked late." Enid catches Rose's look. "No, I honestly did often work late. It's the nature of that sort of business. Lots of deadlines and last-minute scrambles."

"Do you miss it?"

"I try not to think about it, because one thing leads to another and … well, it's best if I don't follow that path." Enid scrapes her plate to get the last of the apple crumble. "And besides, now I have the flora and fauna of the Ashdown Forest to keep me occupied."

"Do you really find that interesting?" asks Rose. "Because honestly, I can't see the appeal."

"I really do."

Enid pulls her specimens towards her. "Let me show you what I found today."

Rose stands up. "I should really do the washing-up." But she can see the flash of hurt in her sister-in-law's eyes, so she sits back down again. "Or the washing-up can wait," she says. "And you can show me what you've discovered and I can pretend to be interested."

MRS. STUART hasn't returned home. Rose heard from a neighbour that she's still in hospital, recovering from her stroke. It's unsettling for Rose to be out on patrol and see Mrs. Stuart's pitch-black house in perfect accordance with the rules of the blackout. It seems wrong for there to be no brightly lit front room shining like a beacon at the top of the road. The rule-breakers are more interesting than the conformers, thinks Rose as she walks past Mrs. Stuart's shadowed house. And you miss the rule-breakers when they're gone.

It is as though everyone has finally understood what is required of them during the blackout, or perhaps with the absence of Mrs. Stuart's bad example, there is nothing to lead anyone else astray. Whatever the reason, for the first night since she became an ARP warden, Rose doesn't have to give a caution. It makes her rounds much shorter than normal. She heads home and, coming up the path to the edge of the forest, laughs out loud when she sees her own cottage glowing with light.

Enid must be absorbed in her nature cataloguing and has forgotten to draw the curtains.

Rose stands in the front garden of her cottage and looks into her sitting room, where Enid lounges on the chesterfield reading a book, her feet pulled up under her. There's a lamp on beside her and another on across the room. Even the electric light in the hallway is blazing.

When she marries Toby, Rose will offer the cottage to Enid. It would be nice for James to come home to someone. It would be nice for the cottage to be lived in. It suits Enid. She looks like she belongs there.

The thought of James makes Rose nervous. She has written to him asking for a divorce, but she hasn't heard back yet. She dreads that letter, and yet there will also be relief in it. She won't have to sneak around anymore. She won't have to pretend. Well, she'll still have to pretend to her parents, but not so much to everyone else.

Enid gets up, switches off the lamp. She's on her way up to bed. There's a looseness to how she moves when she's alone that catches at Rose, makes her breath stop for a moment in her throat. What is it?

It's James. Seeing Enid walk across the room has reminded Rose of James. Their manner is the same. And for the first time since he's been gone, she feels him back and it unnerves her.

THAT NIGHT there's a storm. Enid wakes up to a crash outside the cottage, meets Rose on the landing carrying a torch.

"The electric's gone out," says Rose. "I think a tree might have come down."

The dog shoots past Enid on the staircase, almost knocking her over on her way downstairs.

"Don't let Harris out," Rose warns as they pull on rubber boots at the front door. "She'll bolt in a storm. I made the mistake of letting her out once, and she was gone for three days."

Harris, who seems to have forgotten this memory and her fear of storms, pushes eagerly against their legs when they open the door, and Enid has to knee the dog back inside the hallway and then quickly slam the door to stop her from escaping.

Outside, the wind swirls the tops of the trees and tangles Enid's nightie around her legs. The weak lick of torchlight doesn't reach as far as the gate. Beyond it, the night swells and rages, invisible and noisy.

"I can't see a damned thing," says Enid.

Rose swings the useless torch up towards the roof of the cottage, but the light won't extend that far. "Shall we walk around the house?" she suggests. "You could go one direction, and I will go the other. Just to see if there's a tree fallen on the roof."

Enid takes the left side of the building, starting at the sitting-room window and working her way slowly around to the kitchen door. She keeps one hand on the stone wall, not daring to lose contact with the building as she stumbles through the old flower beds and bits of rubble that border Sycamore Cottage.

Often in London, if she was out after the blackout, Enid would have to negotiate her way through the streets in a similar fashion, trailing her fingers along the iron railings of the park or bumping along the low stone wall outside the terrace of flats on her road. There was always a mix of thrill and terror in this blind fumbling towards home, and when Enid meets Rose at the back of the cottage, she is suddenly flooded with relief.

"Did you see anything?" asks Rose.

"Nothing."

"Must have come down in the lane, then." Rose puts a hand on Enid's arm and can feel how cold her skin is. "Let's go back in," she says. "I'll make some cocoa to warm us up."

ROSE WAKES up early. The sun has not yet risen. She lies in the darkness for a few moments, and then she reaches over and switches on her bedside lamp to see if the electricity is back on. The light haloes out into the room, falling most strongly on the photograph of her and James that stands beside the lamp on the night table.

What Rose remembers of her wedding day is that

there was a heat wave. Her bouquet wilted. Her dress stuck to her body.

She looks closely at the photograph, sees how firmly she's holding on to James's arm, how open his face looks. Why can't she remember that part? Why can't she remember how it felt to stand at the front of the church and Repeat after me?

Rose lays the photograph face down on the night table.

Enid is up when Rose goes downstairs. She is wearing slippers, a wool skirt, and at least two cardigans. She looks a bit like a madwoman who's escaped from the asylum.

"The lights are back on," says Rose. "I thought I might go out and see what the damage is."

She takes the dog with her. There's still the smell of rain, even though the morning is dry. There's another smell too. Rose stops and sniffs the air. Harris, who's disconcerted that Rose is behaving like a dog, stops and sniffs the air as well. It's the smell of green wood, and it belongs to a massive oak that's fallen across the laneway and squashed the garden shed of Linden Cottage. The branches of the tree are cracked and broken, the roots exposed and dripping with earth.

Rose puts her hand gently on the rough bark of the fallen tree, as though she were a nurse feeling the forehead of a sick patient.

When she gets back to the cottage, Enid comes into the hallway to meet her.

"Well?" she asks.

"An oak came down in the lane," says Rose, shucking her boots onto the mat by the door. "I used to collect acorns from that tree when I was a child. It's very old. My grandfather remembered it as being old—that's how old it is. It's so sad it's come down." She hands something to Enid. It's a small twig with a couple of leaves attached. "I thought you might like this for your collection."

Enid is touched. She doesn't have the heart to tell Rose that she isn't collecting mementos but is doing a much more scientific survey of the natural history in the area.

"Thank you." She tucks the twig into the pocket of her cardigan.

"You are coming with me today, aren't you?" asks Rose.

"Yes, of course."

"Good. I'm glad."

Rose is taking Enid to her parents' house for Sunday lunch. Her sister-in-law's presence will be a buffer to any awkward questions about James.

They set off across the heath at noon, Harris bounding along beside them. It's a foggy day, the mist sheathing the dry grass fields, and the dog looks ghostly as she disappears and then reappears ahead of them.

It's a good idea to bring Enid to lunch, but still Rose worries about the event and wishes she didn't have to go, wishes she could just nip down to the Three Bells and spend the day with Toby instead.

"My mother's difficult," she says. "You might not like her."

"Oh, I don't need to like her," says Enid. "I just need her to be a good cook."

But Enid is appalled at Constance's controlling manner at the dinner table. Every item that is lifted off the tablecloth has to be replaced exactly where it was taken from, and if it isn't, Constance quickly moves out a hand to fix the error. They sit in strained silence until the courses are in the process of changing, and then Enid and Frederick bolt for the garden to have a cigarette.

Harris is out there, lying mournfully on the flag-stones, her head between her paws.

"Meals aren't really Constance's forte," says Frederick. He bends down to pat the dog. "She's never been very good at enjoying herself."

"Well, it's hard to learn how to do, isn't it?" says Enid. "I don't think I'm very good at it myself."

"But you probably don't count the number of Brussels sprouts that each person takes and remove from their plate any that exceed the quota."

"What is the quota?"

"Eight."

They wander down to the back of the garden, stand by a mound of dead leaves against the fence.

"For burning," says Frederick. "I save that chore up until I need an excuse to be out of the house for several hours."

Why do you bother? thinks Enid. But she is used to men complaining about their wives and knows that it hardly ever translates into their leaving them. She smokes her cigarette and kicks at the pile of leaves with her foot. The smell that rises from them is loamy and sharp.

"You look like James," says Frederick.

"When we were children, it was hard to tell us apart. I was taller than him for years."

"What is the age difference?"

"I'm two years older." Enid lights another cigarette off the tip of the first. She's not ready to go back inside the house yet. She's not sure how she'll be able to manage the strict rules that will undoubtedly exist around the pudding and the cheese and biscuits.

"Have you heard from him? Rose is short on news." Frederick follows Enid's example and lights a second cigarette from the fag end of his first.

"No. I've had nothing either." Enid thinks about how the post arrives twice a day in the caged letter-box inside the cottage door. Many days she is the one to collect the post. She can't remember there being a single letter from James in the weeks she's been at Sycamore Cottage.

Frederick sighs, and the sigh turns into a long, protracted cough. He sputters to a close, wipes his watery eyes with a handkerchief.

"Funny," he says.

"What's funny?"

"Rose never mentions him anymore."

~~~

"Was it excruciating for you?" asks Rose as they walk back over the heath. The mist has cleared and the forest reveals itself again, the muted colours of the heather and the bracken soothing to the eye.

"Your mother's awful," says Enid.

"Yes." Rose feels guilty for being disloyal. "But my father's all right."

"He's a tattler."

"She's hard to live with."

"But he married her, so he chose his fate."

Rose is silent for a few moments. Harris sprints past them, Clementine at her heels.

"But when he married her, he didn't know his fate," Rose suggests.

"Debatable," says Enid. "But don't mind me. You can't expect me to be a supporter of marriage, can you?"

"No, I suppose not."

They walk on. Enid notices a bog asphodel and the differences in the two varieties of gorse in their path.

"But when you marry," says Rose, "you don't know anything. You don't know how it will turn out, or what you'll feel later."

"Rose." Enid puts a hand on her arm, stops her.

"What's going on? Why hasn't James written in so long? Has something happened to him?"

"Why is it James everyone is always so worried about and not me?" Rose shakes off Enid's arm and bolts down the path, and the dogs, excited by her sudden running, give chase across the field.

When Enid gets back to the cottage, Rose isn't there but the dogs are. Enid tidies up the dishes and sits on the chesterfield reading.

At midnight Rose still hasn't returned, so Enid lets the dogs out one final time, switches off the lights in the cottage, and climbs the stairs to bed. In her room, she takes out her pad of writing paper and pen and begins a letter to her brother.

Dear James,

Are you well? I haven't had a letter from you in ages, and it seems that Rose has not heard from you either.

James, if something has happened, please let me know. I worry about your welfare, even if when I write I pretend that all is well with you, and that everything is as it should be.

~~~

THERE'S WIND against the panes again tonight, a whistle and shudder as it roams the trees outside the pub.

Rose squeezes closer to Toby.

"I'm not going home," she says. "I'm just going to stay the night with you."

"What about Enid?"

"I don't care about the pretense anymore. Besides, she's close to guessing that something's up. She said as much to me today."

"Good," says Toby. "It's better to have no secrets. Lies are always harder to manage than the truth."

But in the morning when Rose wakes up, scrunched against the wall of the single bed, her hands numb and her neck aching, she feels terrible for not being home to feed the hens and tend to the dogs, even to have her morning cup of tea with Enid. Once her sister-in-law finds out the truth about Rose, she'll have no more to do with her, and Rose has liked having Enid around these past weeks, has depended on her company. No, she doesn't prefer the truth at all. She just wants to continue on with the lie.

The swallows have already left their nest under the eaves for their morning's work of catching insects. They make passes against the glass, their agile bodies slicing the air, the shapes they make so daring and complicated.

"If our fighter pilots could fly like that, we'd win the war in a fortnight," says Toby.

"How long have you been awake?"

"Just for a few moments." He stretches his arms overhead and Rose nestles down beside him, lying across him, feeling the silky patch of blond hair in the centre of his chest against her cheek, not unlike the feeling of lying with her face pressed into Harris.

"I'm worried about what Enid will think," she says. "What if she waited up for me last night?"

"She probably slept right through. You can sneak back up the road now, and she'll be none the wiser."

But Enid is waiting for Rose when she gets home, pacing up and down in the kitchen, furious.

"I imagined all sorts of terrible things," she says. "You had no right to rush off like that without telling me when you'd be back. How was I to know something awful hadn't happened to you? And what about your blackout patrol last night? Did you even do that?"

"Oh, no." Rose had completely forgotten about her blackout watch. She sits down at the kitchen table with her head in her hands. "I'm sorry," she says. "I went to stay with a friend for the night."

"Really, Rose," says Enid. "Sometimes you behave as though you're twelve." And with that, she stomps out of the kitchen. A few moments later, Rose hears the front door slam.

Enid marches across the heath for an hour before her anger wears off. She has neglected to bring her books and bags, but that's all right. Enid doesn't feel calm enough to work on her natural history this morning.

Rose is lying to her. There's probably a man at the bottom of it all. A sordid mess, thinks Enid, her anger fired up again. Poor James. But frankly, it's the lying that irks her the most. She had warmed to Rose. They had been good companions of late. The lying makes them seem nothing but strangers.

Time to go, thinks Enid. She'll write to her friend Molly in Bath to see if she can stay with her for a few weeks until she gets herself sorted. There's nothing to be gained from embroiling herself in trouble between her brother and his wife. Nothing to be gained at all.

~~~

Rose comes home the next day to find the cottage quiet and tidy, a short note for her from Enid with a forwarding address in Bath. Upstairs, Enid's bed is stripped, the eiderdown carefully folded at the foot of the mattress, the sheets in the laundry bin.

Rose sits down on the bed. The afternoon sun angles in the small window, sends a shaft of light across the wooden floorboards. Rose follows the light over the boards to the bureau. There, on top of the bureau, is Enid's notebook for her natural history. There's no note to accompany it, but it's clearly been left rather than forgotten. Rose stands at the bureau turning the pages and reading some of the entries. It is not what she had thought Enid was doing, which was to dryly catalogue and describe the various bits of flora she took from the forest on her morning's walk. No, Enid's natural history is not what she'd expected at all.

RED SQUIRREL: *Too plentiful to list all locations, but mainly to be seen in the wooded areas of the forest. Native to England. First appeared at the end of the last ice age, some ten thousand years ago. Can be either right- or left-handed. Once the choice of fur for the nobility, called vair and especially popular as slippers. Cinderella's lost slipper at the ball was made of vair. The prince knew she was from the same class as him because he also had red squirrel slippers. In the translation from French to English, the word was changed to verre, and the slipper went from squirrel fur to glass.*

NIGHTINGALE: *I have heard two while I've been here. One in the wooded area near the Wealdway, and another near Gills Lap. Melodious songbird. Distantly related to the robin. It has been the inspiration for a great deal of poetry and song, most recently the popular tune "A Nightingale Sang in Berkeley Square." Oliver was fond of that song. He would often sing it to me.*

RED ADMIRAL BUTTERFLY: *Seen all over the heath, particularly in areas where there is an abundance of wildflowers. Named after and known for their "admirable" colours. They are unusual in that they fly at night. Most butter-*

flies are active only in daylight hours. Migratory. Territorial. Not afraid of humans. Short-lived. Some cultures believe them to be the transformation of human souls.

COMMON DARTER: *Spotted over the more boggy areas of the forest. Born under water, but spending their lives in the air. The last dragonfly species to be seen at the end of summer, and still alive well into October. Mate over water. Often used as a way to explain death. The underwater nymph bears no resemblance to the dragonfly it becomes, and exchanges one world for another. It cannot communicate to the other nymphs it left behind because they won't recognize the new form it has taken.*

TOAD: *Found in the low-lying boggy areas of the forest, and near the little stream that runs through the Five Hundred Acre Wood. Toads walk rather than hop like frogs. Can live up to forty years. Eat what is dark and in motion. Shed their skin and consume it, rather than simply moving from it as a snake will. They will instinctively return to the same pond as their ancestors. Here they will hibernate for the winter, emerging each spring as though returning from the land of the dead.*

BELL HEATHER: *Simply everywhere. This and the bracken were the first plants I saw when I stepped out onto the forest for the first time. Once used to stuff mattresses, because when dried it was not only cushiony but fragrant as well. Also used for animal bedding. The flowers are bell-shaped, hence the name.*

AGRIMONY: *Near the roadside hedgerows. A yellow flower spike that is pretty but followed by a seed casing of burrs. During medieval times, it was thought to be a cure for internal bleeding when combined with pounded frogs. Also used to detect witches, although I'm not sure how. Invasive. Produces a yellow dye. Can be brewed, and when drunk will produce a merciful dreamless sleep.*

Swallow

TOBY GETS HIS ORDERS AT THE BEGINNING OF August. Rose tries to be cheerful about it, even though she feels nothing but dread at his leaving. He comes to the cottage on the morning he is to take the train to the air base to join his squadron. There's barely an hour before the train leaves, not enough time to go upstairs to bed, or even to sit down in the kitchen for a cup of tea. They stand in the downstairs hallway with their arms around each other for most of the hour.

"Promise me you'll come back," says Rose.

"I promise."

"Here. That you'll come back here, to me."

"I promise."

Toby's suitcase waits by the door. Rose can see it over his shoulder, standing on the mat like a patient dog.

"Shall I walk with you to the station?" she asks.

"No. That would be painful," says Toby. "I'd like to leave just like any other time I've left. I'll walk down the road and think about walking back up it again. In no time at all."

"I'll come to the top of the path with you, then," she says.

"No. Just walk me to the door."

They stand at the door for a few moments, leaning against each other. Toby reaches into his pocket.

"This is for you," he says, handing Rose a small object.

It's a rabbit's foot, the severed part where it once attached to the rabbit's leg wrapped tightly in copper wire.

"I cut it off the rabbit the dogs caught," says Toby. "Seemed a shame to waste the corpse. It will bring you luck while I'm gone."

Rose closes her hand around the rabbit's foot. She can feel the bones in the foot and the little ticky-tack nails of the dead animal as they dig into the flesh on her palm. The foot, dead, feels no different than it would have alive.

She hands it back to him. "You take it. You'll need the luck more than I will."

"But I made it for you."

"Well, make sure I get it back, then."

"That's a promise." Toby drops it into his pocket, kisses her one last time, opens the door, and then is gone.

ROSE IS lonely without Toby in the village and Enid in the house. She mopes around with the dogs, forgets to eat or collect the eggs from the hens, and lingers on her patrols at night, watching people in their lighted houses for a long time before cautioning them to close the curtains, as though their lives are a play staged entirely for her benefit.

Toby writes from the air base where he's been posted, and then again to say he's being sent out on active duty as a navigator. He tells her not to worry. He tells her that he loves her.

James doesn't write at all. Rose has never heard from him after she sent him the letter asking for a divorce. James doesn't write. Enid doesn't write. Toby writes again to say how much he misses her.

Loneliness is sometimes cured by visiting people, and sometimes it's made worse by the same thing. It's often hard to know what course of action to take, but Rose avoids company in case she will hate it, preferring to slouch around the cottage, moving from one meaningless task to the next.

She sometimes reads Enid's natural history in the long stretch of evening between supper and ARP patrol. It comforts her and brings Enid's voice, momentarily, back into Sycamore Cottage.

On an early August morning, Rose is sitting in the kitchen having a cup of tea. The door is open because Harris has gone outside and it's easier when she can come back in herself. Harris and Clementine both have the annoying habit of sitting in front of a closed door, waiting for it to open, not announcing their presence to the person on the other side of the door by scratching or barking.

Rose sits at the table. The door is half open. The warm air from outside blows into the room, carrying with it the scent of roses and the rinsed-fresh smell of morning.

A bird flies into the kitchen. It passes above the table, and then circles back and lands in front of Rose. It is a swallow, its forked tail a glossy bluish black.

The swallow sits on the table, and then it seems to fall asleep, hunched down in its cape of feathers. Rose dares not move. The bird is only inches away from her right hand. It sleeps and Rose remains perfectly still at the table, watching it. She wonders if it is one of Toby's swallows from under the eaves at the Three Bells, although that is rather a romantic notion, as there are plenty of swallows around her cottage as well.

The bird sleeps and then it wakes up, shakes itself, and flies back out through the half-open door. There is no way of knowing how long it was on the table. The clock is in the parlour. The swallow could have been there for half an hour or five minutes.

When the bird leaves, Rose feels shaky and gets up. Her tea has gone cold. She looks out the door, but she can't see the swallow or Harris. She goes upstairs and looks from the window in her bedroom, but there's nothing to be seen from there either.

She walks into the sitting room, trying to settle herself, decides to do some mending that has been piling up beside her chair. When she opens the lid of her sewing box, she sees James's unopened letters lying there, on top of the tray of buttons. It seems a very long time ago that she read a letter from her husband, and yet it's probably only been about six weeks. This is the problem with time, thinks Rose. It doesn't follow its own rules. It stretches or compresses at will. It's either a lingering house guest or an escape artist.

James is from another life now, and his letters no longer have any power to hurt or irritate her. She slits open the envelope of the most recent one with a knitting needle. The letter is a single sheet of paper, folded in half. Rose opens it and reads.

Dear Rose,

What I like about bird behaviour is that it follows a cycle. There is mating, breeding, the incubation of the eggs, the birth of the chicks, the flight of the fledglings, the migration of the family. These activities span three seasons, but they speed the seasons forward with a greater urgency than would exist if I were simply observing the changes from spring to summer to autumn that occur in the vegetable garden or the fluctuations in temperature. I appreciate the imperative of the redstart's small and urgent life because it pulls mine along in its wake, and this prison, which becomes so oppressive and apparent to other men, is less so for me because of this.

Studying the birds here has given me purpose, and this has made all the difference. But something happened that has changed everything again. I cannot tell you the details—suffice to say that I thought I was going to die, but I didn't. And this is what I thought, my darling Rose, when I expected to die. I thought about you. I thought about how much I loved you and our life in that little cottage at the edge of the Ashdown Forest. Nothing else mattered in that moment but you. Not my work or my ambitions or my education. Nothing that I owned, or thought, or wished to be. It was only you and the happiness I felt by your side, the great gift of love that you have given me. Nothing else was of any consequence at all.

Toby and his crew are limping back across the Channel in the Wellington on their return from a bombing raid on Cologne. One of their engines has been knocked out by the ack-ack guns, and the remaining engine must have been hit as well because it's losing pressure.

The pilot, Fletcher, is young, but he has nerve and offers a sort of steely calm to his crew that Toby recognizes as barely controlled panic but the more inexperienced chaps take as confidence.

They need to put the plane down before the remaining engine seizes and quits, and the huge weight of the Wellington, really nothing more than a slow-flying bus, crashes to earth.

Toby sits behind Fletcher, drawing and re-drawing his calculations, trying to determine how far they can make it, what air base they should aim for. Up front, the wireless operator, Curtis, waits for Toby to decide on a course of action so he can radio the corresponding wireless operator at whatever base they choose and tell him they need to put down there.

Toby has decided on Penshurst in Kent. It's not far from the coast, and they're already over land now. It's an emergency landing ground, not a regular airfield, and it will suit if they have to make a hard landing.

There's a moment when it all seems possible. Curtis talks to the wireless operator at Penshurst and they're cleared for landing, with an open airfield and full lights on to guide them in. Fletcher has the plane on a corresponding course. Toby can, for the first time since they lost power in the right-hand engine, put his map and pencil aside. The gunners behind him and the observer, Thomas, are quiet but hopeful. The plane, vibrating with the single engine at full throttle, also vibrates with all their prayers and optimism. For that moment—and for that moment only—it seems they will make it down, will stumble from the plane, laughing with relief at their close call and slapping each other on the back as they head to the mess for a well-earned pint.

But that moment closes and another one opens. The new moment contains the information that the functioning engine is losing oil pressure quickly now. The leak must have increased.

"We won't make it to Penshurst," says Fletcher. "We need to put her down now."

Toby grabs for his map. Thomas, hearing what the pilot has said, is mumbling, "Fuck, fuck, fuck," into the back of Toby's head.

"How fast?" Toby asks. "How fast are we losing pressure? How much time do we have?"

"Minutes," says Fletcher grimly. "Find us an airfield, Halliday."

But minutes won't take them close enough to anything. Toby wipes the sweat from his forehead, finds it hard to keep himself from repeating Thomas's incantation of fear.

And then he sees where they are, not from the air—where it is all, in daylight, a blur of greens and browns, the pretty patchwork of rural England rolling out beneath the plane—but instead from the ground. The town of East Grinstead with its twisty cobbled streets. The long hill down into Forest Row. The road rising up to Rose's cottage, and the flat heath beyond.

"The forest," he says. "You can put her down on the forest. It's flat enough. It's as good as any airfield."

"Ashdown Forest?"

"Yes. It will work." In his mind, Toby strides across the flat open space, turns, and waves his hand to the plane he is in. "It's heath. Hardly any trees."

"Will do," says Fletcher. He pushes the control column forward and the nose of the plane tilts downwards.

"Damn the blackout," says Toby. It's a clear night, but there are no lights visible from East Grinstead. And if Rose is out doing her job, there will be no lights to guide them in towards Forest Row either. He has to trust his numbers, trust that the angle they are cutting through the darkness will bring them right over the village, down over Rose's cottage, and safely onto the flat heath beyond.

The plane shudders with the noise of the one working Rolls-Royce engine, and then it is silent and Thomas's *fuck, fuck, fuck* is its own engine, drawing them forward to their doom.

Fletcher works the toggle for the engine. Nothing. The plane descends.

"Brace yourselves," he yells to his crew. And then, when he looks at the airspeed indicator and realizes how hard they will crash down, he adds, "I'm sorry. I'm so sorry."

The pilot always thinks it is his fault, thinks there was something else he could have done to save them. Toby remembers this from the last time he was in a plane that went down. He reaches forward, grasps Fletcher by the shoulder, wants to say something reassuring, but as it turns out, there is no time for any more words.

Toby wakes up and feels warm. He moves his left arm, but the sharp pain when he does this tells him that it's broken. He turns his head and sees the Wellington on fire about two hundred yards away. The heat from the fire warms the whole left side of his body. The fire pops and crackles as it undoes the plane, turning it back from a bird into a machine made of wood and fabric. From somewhere beyond the fire, Toby can hear a man moaning, and it takes him several moments to realize that the moaning man is himself. He tries to move his legs, to curl them under him and stand up, but he can't seem to feel them. He tries to call out, but his voice is dry and small, like a child's. It falls off into the darkness, barely reaching past the edge of his body.

His good arm feels around him, his hand clutching at the dry clumps of grass he lies on. Overhead, the stars burn in their sockets. Suddenly he is very cold and his teeth chatter in his skull.

And then, out of the night, from the opposite direction to the burning Wellington, come two white angels to take him up to heaven. He shakes his head. No, it can't be. He shakes his head and the angels transform into dogs. Harris and Clementine, racing across the heath towards him. When he calls out, even with his small voice, they hear him.

The dogs lick his face, which Toby realizes is wet with either tears or blood. The dogs lick his face, and then they lie down, one on either side of him, pressing their bodies close so that he is no longer cold. He reaches out with his working hand and touches the head of the dog lying on his right. It's all fine now, he thinks. The fire flickers in the grate, and the dogs are lying with him on the floor of Rose's cottage, and any moment now she will come and lead him upstairs to bed.

WHEN ROSE first opens her eyes in the morning, she forgets about having read James's letter the night before. The room is quiet. The first light at the window is weak through the curtains. She remembers a sound in the night. She moves her feet under the blankets. A dream, perhaps, or a storm. She stretches her arms above her head. And then she remembers the contents of the letter and feels ill.

Downstairs she opens the front door to look at the morning, and there on the steps are the dogs. They don't rush her with enthusiasm as they usually do. They don't make a move at all, and Rose puts a hand out to make sure that they're real, that they're not part of her dream. She puts a hand on Harris's head, and Harris drops something on the stone tiles by Rose's feet.

It's the rabbit's foot with the bit of copper wire twisted around the top. It's the rabbit's foot that Toby had given her, and that she had made him take back, had made him take with him, for luck.

1950

Wild Horse

ENID GETS OFF THE BUS AT THE END OF THE LINE. There are several houses poised on the edge of a cliff, too few to be called a village. It looks like the houses have just roosted there, like birds, and will fly away at any moment.

It's windy when Enid steps from the bus, so windy that it knocks her suitcase against her legs and tries to rip the cardigan from her shoulders. The bus exhales and moves off. Enid looks around, thinking he hasn't come, but there he is, standing stiffly beside a telephone pole. He's wearing a suit.

They walk towards each other at the same time, embrace awkwardly. He pats her back. She knocks her face against his collarbone.

"You dressed up for my arrival," says Enid. "I'm touched."

"Don't flatter yourself. It was either this or my holey green jumper and torn grey flannels. I don't have much company, and the birds don't care that I look a fright." James takes Enid's suitcase from her. "Is this all you have?"

"I travel light. My flat was bombed in the war, remember. I lost everything."

"Oh, come on. Surely you've replaced most of it by now."

"You'd be surprised how little is really important."

"No, I wouldn't." James strides ahead of her, then calls back over his shoulder, "Wait until you see where I'm taking you. It's a very minimal life out here. Big change from London."

Enid had expected her brother to fetch her in a motor car, and she's more than a little disappointed to be taken instead on a forced march along a rutted dirt track for what seems like miles, trotting after James's back as he stalks away from her through the fields. When she tries to call out for him to wait, the wind tears the words right out of her mouth and shreds them into meaningless syllables. She finally gives up trying to make him have any compassion for her and trails along behind him, falling farther and farther back with each step, stoking a murderous rage that erupts when he eventually comes to a stop outside a low whitewashed cottage on the edge of a cliff.

"You could have waited for me"—she strains to be heard above the roar of the wind—"instead of being such a bloody idiot!"

James just pushes open the unlocked cottage door. "You're soft from your city life," he says. "You need to toughen up." He steps into the dark interior of the cottage and Enid follows, her skirts twisted by the wind and her hair so tousled that she's sure she will have more success chopping if off than getting a brush through it again any time soon.

The building is very simple. Two rooms downstairs, barely distinguishable from each other, although one has a cooker and therefore must be the kitchen. There's a table and chairs in that room as well. In the other room there's a fireplace and a chesterfield, a few shelves of books. The floors are uneven. Enid walks two steps into the kitchen and trips twice.

"It was a shepherd's hut," says James. "I've spruced it up a bit."

"How? By moving the sheep outdoors?" Enid still feels angry about the long walk from the bus.

James drops her suitcase and jams his hands into his trouser pockets. "Well," he says, "I suppose it doesn't look like much after London. I suppose it does seem a bit squalid."

"No, it's fine."

"You'll probably be wanting to light out of here as quickly as possible. Next bus back."

"No, I won't," says Enid. "It's just been a tiring day, and I wasn't expecting such a long walk at the end of it."

"Yes, of course." His politeness is a cover for hurt feelings, as always. His adult behaviour remarkably the same as when they were children.

It's been six months since she last saw her brother, and this is the first time she's visited him at the observatory. Their last visit, he came up to London to meet her. Enid doesn't want to be angry with him, even though she still feels angry. She puts a hand on his arm and squeezes. He feels thin through his suit jacket. Her fingers close on bone.

"Show me the rest, James. I'd like to see it all. Show me where you do your work."

There are two small bedrooms upstairs, pinched under the eaves. No WC in the house, or running water. There's a dug well in the yard back of the kitchen and an earth closet tacked onto the outside wall of the sitting room—although "sitting room" seems too gracious a word for what is merely an extension of the kitchen.

After depositing her suitcase in one of the bedrooms, James takes Enid back outside and walks her to the edge of the cliff.

"Three hundred feet straight down," he says.

She holds on to his arm to peer over the edge, the wind a strong hand at her back, trying to push her over. The waves below are white threads in a sheet of blue. The rocky beach is strewn with boulders from the sheer walls of the cliff face.

"God, James," says Enid.

"I know. Seems like the end of the earth, doesn't it?"

"Good thing you're not a sleepwalker."

A gull rises on the wind, white and angular, banking above them and gliding smoothly away.

"Manx gannet," says James. "There's a huge population here. Also large populations of storm petrels and puffins, three kinds of gulls, the wheatear, chough, skylark, and oystercatcher."

"You're busy, then?" They step away from the edge of the cliff, walk back towards the cottage.

"I'm the only observer here. There's a fellow comes to spell me off every once in a while, but mostly it's just me."

"Are you writing another book?"

James nods as he pushes open the cottage door for them. "Seabirds. It seemed to make sense to group them, rather than focus on them individually, like I did for the redstart."

"It still amazes me," says Enid, "that you wrote that book while you were a prisoner of war."

"What else was I to do there? It was good to have a project."

James closes the door behind them, and the silence in the kitchen, after the noise of the wind, is deafening for the moment it takes to adjust to it.

"Do you think much about the camp?"

"Not if I can help it. Not unless someone brings it up." James rubs his hands together, blows on them to warm them. "I could heat us up some soup for lunch, if you'd like?"

"That would be nice."

He lights the stove under a large tin can. The label has been torn off and it takes Enid a moment to realize that James is using the can as a pot. She looks around the kitchen and sees other tin cans in various sizes, all without lids. There are no actual pots or mugs visible on the open shelves.

"Can't you afford a saucepan?" she asks.

"This works just as well. Nothing wrong with it." James lifts the tin can from the hob using the sleeve of his sweater.

"Can't you afford an oven mitt?"

He doesn't answer.

They eat at the rough wooden kitchen table, with its gouges and knife marks. James must use it as a cutting board, thinks Enid, but she doesn't ask him. The way he lives in this cottage seems harsh and hard, but she doesn't say this either. She sips the bland beef-and-barley soup and praises its taste. She chews the stale rind of bread he gives her and remarks on its pleasing texture. She tells him he looks good for all the fresh air and country living, instead of saying that he's too thin and noting that his hands shake when he butters his bread. James, on the other hand, isn't as charitable, or as careful in his comments.

"You look an awful lot like Mummy," he says.

Their mother, dead now, was stout and square, with a miserable downcast expression and a rather frightening receding hairline.

"That's a terrible thing to say."

"Is it?" James shrugs. "She wasn't so bad."

"Maybe not as a person, but to look at?"

James shrugs again. "I miss them," he says. "We're all alone now, Eenie. No children to follow us. When we die, that's it for our little family. Do you ever think about that?"

"Yes, I do." Enid has been largely shocked by her passage into middle age. She has trouble recognizing her body when she passes a shop window or glances in the mirror. She doesn't resemble her younger self at all, and worse, she doesn't look anything like she imagines herself to look.

But she still feels like the person she used to be, and she tells herself that this is the important thing, that this is what matters most.

"It's awful what happens to us, Eenie," says James, getting up abruptly from the table.

"What happens to us?" asks Enid, but James has clattered his dishes into the sink and has moved off into the other room. She follows him. He's standing with his back to her, and when she gets closer he turns around. He has a glass full of amber liquid in his hand. Scotch, she guesses. He holds it out to her.

"Bit early in the day, isn't it?" she says.

James downs the drink, starts to pour another.

Enid puts a hand on his shoulder. "Show me your work," she says. "I'd like to see your book in progress."

"It's all in the room where you're sleeping," says James. "You can look at it any time you like." He collapses onto the chesterfield, a cloud of dust rising when he sits down.

It's cold in the room, in the cottage, in Wales. It's only September, but it might as well be winter.

"I'll make us a fire," says Enid, getting down on her hands and knees in front of the grate. At least he has seen fit to get in a supply of logs and kindling. She wrings some sheets of newspaper into twists, lays the twigs on top. "Matches?"

James digs into his trouser pocket and tosses her a box.

The fire makes everything seem better. Enid sits on the chesterfield beside her brother, her feet curled under her for warmth, even though she's still got her shoes on.

"Are you still working at that magazine, then?" asks James.

"Yes. I like it. There's always a deadline. Keeps me on my toes."

"And no romance?"

"I'm happy on my own."

"Wouldn't you like some nice retired colonel in Tunbridge Wells?" James grimaces in an attempt to smile, and Enid can see that whatever hole he fell into, he's climbing back out now.

"Just shoot me," she says, "if I ever find a retired colonel from Tunbridge Wells appealing."

James sips his second drink. His hands have stopped shaking.

"Do you ever see her?" he asks. "Does she ever write to you?"

"Who?"

"Rose."

Enid lays her head on his bony shoulder. He flinches, but then he yields, and she can feel his body unclench a little. "Not for years, James," she says. "Not since I lived with her that summer."

"Did you ever see them together, she and Halliday?"

"No."

The fire gains strength, crawls up the logs. The room brightens accordingly.

"I think I guessed, though," Enid says. "She was always coming and going, all flustered, forgetting things. Always late. I was a bit naive, in retrospect. It was actually quite obvious."

"She was in love, wasn't she?" says James. "With Toby Halliday. You know, I don't think she ever really loved me. How could she have, if she went off with him?"

"You can't assume she didn't love you," says Enid. She suddenly sees Rose bursting into the kitchen, looking healthy and happy, her big white dog at her heels. "She was young. You were far away. It's the arithmetic of war." She lifts her head from his shoulder. "You know that Halliday died? Crashed on the forest?" They haven't spoken of this in ages, not since the divorce, and Enid can't remember what her brother does and doesn't know.

"Of course I know that." James gets up, pours another drink, and sits back down beside his sister. "I was happy when I heard about it."

"Do you still feel like that? All these years later?"

"Yes. No. I don't know." James sips his Scotch. "Time doesn't really soften anything. Memories heave up, you know. Still sharp."

"Forgetting takes practice," says Enid. "You have to work at it."

She thinks of how she doesn't really remember Oliver at all. After years of pushing the thoughts of him away, now she doesn't think of him. If you pretend to feel a certain way, eventually you do feel that way. That has been a surprisingly pleasant lesson to learn in life.

"Maybe you're too isolated here," she says delicately. "Maybe you have too much time to brood on the past."

"My work is solitary work," says James. "I can't help that."

"Yes, but do you have to do it so far away from people?"

"Birds don't like crowds. They're wild creatures. They can put up with my presence, just barely, but they wouldn't tolerate a group of us. Solo observation has always been the most effective way to study them." James turns to look at his sister. "I'm not just brooding here, Enid," he says. "I'm working."

When Enid goes up to bed that evening, she sees that he's been telling her the truth. With a candle (for there is no electric light in the cottage), she looks through his pages and pages of notes, each written in a meticulous, tidy hand, all dated, and the dates trailing each other in reliable succession. Perhaps it is her presence that has upset his balance, made him think about the past? Perhaps he is not this way every night? She tells herself these things, sitting on the edge of the creaky single bed in the dark, but she does not altogether believe them.

JAMES DOESN'T mention Rose the next morning. He makes soft-boiled eggs for them and they eat the rest of the hard bread, which is much better toasted. After breakfast, James takes Enid on a walk through the fields and along the cliff path. She sits with him while he watches the gannets scale and descend the air along the cliff face. She is pleased to see that he still has the binoculars she gave him for a wedding gift, and that, from the worn look of the carrying strap, he uses them almost every day at the observatory.

Enid has brought a blanket from her bed to wrap herself in. She is determined not to be as cold as she was yesterday. They have a flask of tea with them, but she doesn't want to drink it too soon and then want it much more later on, when it's already been consumed.

It's so hard to get life right, she thinks, pulling the blanket tight around her shoulders. All the small balances are impossible to strike most of the time. And then there are the larger choices. It's hopeless. She might as well be one of those gannets, tossed about by the gusts of wind that drive up from the Atlantic.

"Do you think they're flying?" she asks James, who's busy making notes beside her. "Or are they just being buffeted about? I mean, do you think they're going where they want to go?"

"More or less. They're better at it than we are, I'd say."

He has been thinking the same thing as she has, and this makes Enid feel close to her brother again, as though time has not come between them, as though they are still children on the farm. Back then, every day was an adventure they embarked on together.

"I remember you as a little boy, Jimmy, lying on your back in the fields, watching the birds and making up stories about them for me."

James looks at her. "Did I do that? I don't remember." He puts his pencil down. "I hope they were good stories."

"Very good." Although Enid is hard pressed to recall any of her younger brother's tales now, she does remember her delight at hearing them.

Two gannets circle their heads and then slide sideways on a current of air, disappearing over the edge of the cliff.

"Look," James says. "The gannets that fly on course and the ones that get thrown about by the wind mostly end up in the same place, so perhaps effort doesn't matter, isn't what ensures survival."

THAT NIGHT, James drinks less. They sit on the chesterfield by the fire, and he writes up his notes for the day, drawing little pictures of the birds in the margins of his notebook.

"If I draw them, I get a better sense of them," he says when Enid peers over his arm to look at the miniature ink birds arcing off the edges of the page. "I can feel their bodies, rather than just seeing them."

Her brother's notebook and his drawings make Enid think back to her own collection of specimens from the Ashdown Forest.

"Did you ever see the little natural history I made of the forest?" she asks. "I left it for you at the cottage."

"Did you?" James looks up, then looks back down and finishes drawing the right wing of a gannet. "That's a shame. I never went back to that cottage, and Rose didn't include it with the things she sent on to me in Bristol."

James had come home from the war and gone to stay near their parents while he waited for the divorce to go through.

"Did she ever apologize?" Enid cannot believe that Rose wouldn't have had regrets about divorcing

James. After all, Toby Halliday was dead, and it seemed he was the sole reason for the divorce.

"She wrote and said some nonsense about making a mistake," says James, the strokes of his pen nib making a scraping noise as he shades in the wing of the gannet.

"Maybe it was a mistake? Maybe she had regrets?"

"Too late, Eenie, even if that was what she felt. You can't undo actions with words."

"What good are words, then?" For Enid thinks that this is precisely what words are for—to change what was awful into something you can live with. She has made a neat story of her affair with Oliver Matheson. It is a story fuelled by desperate loneliness (hers) and rampant opportunism (his), set within an atmosphere of fear and unease (the start of war). It makes sense to her to understand it this way, and it's much easier to live with than her earlier version, which involved a lot of guilt and shame on her part, and had Oliver in the role of tragic hero, dying in her arms during the bombing raid—which isn't how it actually happened, but somehow became how it happened. Enid has even told the story out loud several times, and she is surprised to find that something that played such a large part in her younger life takes only the length of one gin and tonic to disclose.

THAT NIGHT she lies in her bed listening to the wind howl outside the cottage. It seems to rise from the ocean and tear across the fields, like a wild animal. There are no trees around the stone building. It is the tallest thing in the landscape, and so the wind wants to destroy it, circles it wildly, trying to pull it apart.

The windows leak air around their frames, and the breeze inside her bedroom is strong enough to ruffle Enid's hair, which is spread out on her pillow. She feels she is on the topmast of a ship, being blown apart in a gale. The little cottage seems to belong more to the Atlantic than to the land it sits on. She imagines it pitching about on a stormy sea, heading out on the choppy waters for the coast of Ireland.

The noise of the wind at first keeps her awake, then puts her to sleep, and finally wakes her again.

The moaning grows so loud that Enid, slowly coming to consciousness, realizes it is not the wind at all.

She opens James's door without knocking.

"James?" He is curled up in a ball on his mattress. His covers are stripped off and strewn on the floor. He is rocking and holding his knees, rocking and moaning. She can't tell if he's asleep or awake.

"James?" Enid walks over and gingerly lays a hand on his shoulder.

He twitches awake and sits bolt upright.

"It's all right. I'm here. It's all right." Enid rubs his arm, his back. He's shaking, and his thick flannel pyjamas are soaked with sweat. "Did you have a nightmare? Do you want to talk about it?"

"Best not," says James, his voice a hoarse whisper.

It's colder in James's room than it is in hers. His room fronts onto the cliffs, is directly in the path of the ocean wind.

"Well, let's get you into some dry clothes, then. Do you have other pyjamas?"

James nods.

"Which drawer?" Enid walks over to the small bureau that stands under the window. She lights the candle on top.

"Middle," says James. "Eenie, how about fetching me a drink?"

"Water?" Enid comes back with the pyjamas.

"Whisky."

Enid gets James his drink while he changes into the dry pyjamas. She has no idea how or where he does laundry, but she bundles his wet pyjamas up efficiently and puts them out on the landing for now.

She sits on the bed beside her brother while he finishes his drink.

"I'm sorry for talking so much about Rose," she says.

"It's not Rose," says James.

"What is it, then?"

"Fetch me another?" James holds out his empty glass to her, and Enid reluctantly takes it, goes back downstairs, and returns with a second tumbler of Scotch for him. His drinking has certainly increased since the last time she was with him.

He takes a sip, then another, cradling the glass in both of his hands. He's tucked up in bed now, looking like an invalid. Enid remembers that when they were children, they would get all the same illnesses, but James would always get much sicker than she would, lingering about in bed days after she was already better and playing outdoors again.

"It's the camp, I suppose," he says after a while.

"I thought you said the camp was tolerable and the Germans didn't treat you that badly."

"That's mostly true. I could concentrate on my study of the redstarts and block out everything else in the first camp. The second one, too, had birds to watch, although it was more crowded." He pauses. "It's the terror of being locked up, I suppose—of not knowing what is going to happen next. At the time I didn't think of it that way, but that's how it comes back to me now." He pauses again, takes another drink. "A young man from my bunkhouse was shot while escaping. He was no more than a boy. Another of the men was shot right in front of me. Carmichael. He'd been whistling and his lips were still pursed when he fell. His eyes looked so surprised. Bits of his brain splattered my shirt. That's how close I was to him."

"That's awful."

"Right after that I was taken from the camp to be shot, or at least that's what I thought." James drains the last of the whisky. "But I was removed from the camp by the Kommandant so he could show me a flock of cedar waxwings. It was an act of friendship, but I misread it. And now it crawls back to me in the middle of the night—the certainty that I was going to die, the feeling of a fear so overwhelming that I can't seem to get out of its way when it comes for me. And the surprised face of Carmichael as he fell dead in his garden. And the poor murdered body of Ian Davis. And then, of course, there's Rose."

"I knew it had to do with Rose."

"That day I thought I was to be killed, I never loved her more. And she was already with Toby Halliday then." James laughs. "I suppose if it gets too bad, it's only a hundred and eighty-seven steps to the edge of the cliff."

"Don't say that." A pause. "Why have you counted them?"

Her brother doesn't reply.

Enid takes the glass from his hands, sets it on the floor to try to make him forget about asking for another drink.

"I wish you would come back with me to the city," she says.

"I don't like the city. It's too big and noisy. There are no birds there."

"What about transferring to an observatory in a bigger community?"

"Perhaps." James folds his hands across his chest. "But not until I've finished my book on the seabirds."

"How far along are you?"

"Halfway through."

"Finish it quickly, then, James." Enid squeezes his hand. "Please. I worry about you out here. It's not good for you to be so alone."

"I will finish it quickly. I will. I promise." He sounds like the little boy he used to be. Jimmy, telling her stories on his back under the low West Country sky, or trussed up in bed recovering from measles, carefully studying the black-and-white photos in his pocket guide to British birds.

ON ENID's last day with her brother, she wakes up early and washes out James's pyjamas at the pump in the yard, pegging them onto a sagging piece of rope running from the corner of the cottage to the roof of the earth closet. The pyjamas flap about like flags in the wind for half an hour and then dry stiff as cardboard.

"Can I take you shopping today?" Enid asks James when he comes downstairs later that morning. "You have virtually nothing in your larder, and I'd like to see you well provisioned before I leave. I'd like to buy you at least one bloody saucepan. And a kettle."

"It's a walk and a bus ride to the shops," says James.

"I don't mind."

James grumbles about the time away from his gannets, but he actually seems glad when Enid marches him through the shops of the neighbouring village, buying him eggs, cheese, vegetables, a bit of bacon, a small joint of beef, some apples.

"I don't want you to starve," she says. "Because it seems to me that you are starving."

"It's hard to bother with food," admits James, "when the shops are so far away."

"Well, we'll get you some tins as well then, shall we? But promise me you'll throw them out when they're empty."

Enid is all business, and in his long experience of her in this mode, James knows better than to argue. He slouches meekly behind his older sister, carrying the shopping and protesting less and less when she takes out her purse to pay for the items she's buying him.

On the walk back to the cottage, the sun actually comes out for an hour or so and the sombre scrubby fields bask golden in the sudden light.

"It's beautiful," says Enid when the sun transforms the landscape from unruly to hospitable. "I can see why you like it here."

"You're never tempted by the country?" James walks beside her, eating an apple, ambling slowly along, not racing ahead as he had on the day she arrived. He's more relaxed, thinks Enid, and she's pleased with that thought. "You used to like living on the farm."

"I was a child then. Childhood is always romantic, no matter where one spends it." Enid moves her hair out of her eyes. "I did like those weeks I spent in your cottage with Rose," she says. "But no. The countryside doesn't offer what the city does."

"And what exactly does the city offer?"

"People, James. People."

"Ah." He takes a bite of his apple. "People are overrated, Eenie. The five years I spent locked up with two thousand men on a few acres of earth was enough humanity to last a lifetime."

There's a movement over the field and they both glimpse it at the same time. A white horse running along the horizon, fast and furious and alone. There is no one leading or trailing it.

"Wild horse," says Enid.

"No such thing here," says James. "It must have escaped from somewhere."

The horse is coming closer to them; it will cross the path they are on a few hundred feet ahead of them.

When it does cross in front of them, they can see that its mane and tail are stuck with burrs and there are several long, bloody scratches scoring its flanks.

"See?" says James. "It must have caught itself on a wire fence when it was pushing through or jumping over."

"Those are bramble scratches," says Enid. "And look how tangled the mane is. That's definitely a wild horse."

"It can't be."

"But it is."

The horse thunders away from them, through the field to the left of the path they are on. It's running hard, as though it is being pursued, even though there's no one running after it.

"It's scared," says James.

"No, it's free," says Enid.

LATER THAT afternoon, James walks Enid back along the path to the bus stop so she can catch the coach that will take her to the train that will, in turn, take her back to London. He carries her suitcase as they tramp through the empty fields. There's no horse to be seen now, no evidence that it was ever there, and James wonders if the horse was real at all. He often thinks he sees things that aren't really there, or else the wind brings voices to his window at night. It is hard to know what to believe, but this is why he likes the birds. He watches them and writes down what they do, and by attaching himself to their purpose, he keeps himself firmly attached to his own reality.

James wishes both that Enid could stay longer and that she'd never come at all. Because now that she's been to see him, he'll miss her, and missing her will open up that hole in him that requires large amounts of whisky to fill. Her absence will be noticeable because her presence was welcome, and her coming to visit has made him realize how lonely he is, and this will be made worse once she leaves.

He wishes he could go to London with her and start again somehow, but he knows he can't. He is over forty, too old to start anything again. He has his work, and most days he can cleave to that, to the rise and fall of the birds' wings, to their strict routines, to the urgent occupancy of their small, short lives. They are predictable and comforting, and he depends on their existence for his own.

The bus puffs up the street. James hands Enid her suitcase.

"Don't be a stranger," he says, trying to smile.

"Don't drink so much." She kisses him on the cheek, squeezes his arm. "Take care of yourself, Jimmy. I'll write to you."

The bus pulls up in front of them and the doors shush open. Enid steps towards them, turns back.

"A letter is a good thing, you know," she says. "Sometimes we can write what we can't say. You could write to Rose."

"I did that once," he says. "It didn't turn out so well." She starts to say something, but he nudges her shoulder. "Go on, Eenie. Don't hold up the driver now."

She waves from her seat inside the bus, and though James means to turn and walk away, he ends up standing in the road, waving at the bus until it is long out of sight.

ONCE JAMES saw a redstart outside the observatory. It was a migrant, probably blown off course by a storm, and it sheltered for two days under the eaves of his bedroom, perching on the window ledge before flying away to spend the winter in Africa. He wondered if it was a descendant of one of his redstarts in Germany, if that was where it had originated. He wondered if it had memory in some part of its bodily cells of him watching the redstarts in the prison camp and this is why it had come directly there, to him.

This is why James likes birds—because they are all possibility. They make a line in the air, the invisible line of their flight, and this line can join up with other lines or lead somewhere entirely new. All you have to do is believe that the line exists and learn how to follow it.

And sometimes life will make this same invisible line for him, make him see where he came from, what he is attached to. Enid flew up out of his past, and he can follow the line of her all the way back to the farm-house in the West Country, to the smell of animals in the barn and his mother's bread baking in the kitchen, to that point in time when he was Jimmy Hunter, a boy who believed in the goodness and possibility of absolutely everything.

Marsh Gentian

Enid goes straight to the magazine, even though it's early evening by the time she gets back to London.

But they're going to press next week, and as always, there's a mad scramble to meet the deadline. And even though it's almost seven o'clock, all the lights are burning on the third floor of the building where the *Country Ways* offices are housed, and practically every single employee of the magazine is still hard at work.

Enid works in the art department of *Country Ways* as a paste-up artist. It is her job to receive the finished galleys from typography, wax them, and fix them to the paste-up boards so they can be photographed and made into plates, then run off on the printing press and gathered together as the pages of the magazine. *Country Ways* is a complex mix of text and advertisements, photographs and illustrations. Each of these things has to be carefully put down on the boards according to the wishes of the designer. Being a paste-up artist requires a good eye and steady hands, as the text has to go down straight and there are lots of instances—captions of photos, for example—where individual lines of type have to be carefully cut out and even more carefully laid into position. It is finicky work, but Enid likes it. There is satisfaction in getting the pages loaded up with their text and images. This is also the point at which Enid reads the magazine, never bothering with it when it is actually finished and out on the newsstands. She reads the articles as she lays them out on her drafting table in her little corner of the art department, with the window at her back that looks down onto the moving tide of people and the tops of the London buses in the streets below.

Country Ways tries to speak fully to the inhabitants of the countryside, men and women alike, although even with so many men so recently back from the war, the audience for the magazine remains largely female. The magazine ambitiously tries to address every one of Britain's roughly twenty-five million women. It seems to be working, as the number of new readers increases with each monthly issue. Now in its eighth year of production, *Country Ways* continues to be popular. The people of Britain can't ignore the effects of the war and the lingering rationing, but the magazine's heady mix of recipes, knitting patterns, instruction in watercolour, pointers for gardeners, travel recommendations, and jaunts in the countryside is a welcome distraction.

Enid jams a new block of wax in her waxer to melt and goes round the corner to Editorial.

She pokes her head into Margaret's office.

"For the new issue," says Enid, "it's thatched cottages, the marsh violet, plum jam, and the vole. Is that right?"

"I think the vole is in with gardening," says Margaret. She pushes her glasses up her nose, and Enid sees a strip of Elastoplast holding the bridge together. "As in, how to get rid of the vole, not how to understand it."

"Oh, right," says Enid. "The vole is a villain

now." Switch categories, switch context. This was a constant practice at *Country Ways*. There would be the heartfelt story of a lamb raised by hand in one issue and a delicious recipe for lamb stew in the next. "What happened to your glasses?"

"Tripped on something. They flew off my head, and then I stepped on them. Is it very noticeable?" Margaret looks worried.

Enid wavers between lying and telling the truth, but decides to lie. "Hardly at all," she says. "Only if you look directly at your nose."

"Oh, dear." Margaret still seems worried, so Enid ducks out of the younger woman's office and goes back to her drafting table.

The waxer is hot enough now, the block of wax under the roller nicely melted. Enid rolls the back of the first galley for *Country Ways*, cuts it to fit, and sticks it down on the layout board. She skims the article on thatched cottages, finding it boring and needlessly detailed. The plum jam recipe is one she's seen before. Enid is sometimes stirred enough by guilt over her own mother's jam-making prowess to attempt to make preserves herself, but it always ends in disappointment. Her jam, no matter what recipe she follows, is too sticky or too thin, too thick to spread easily on toast or running off the edges onto the plate.

Recently, *Country Ways* has run a series on botanical illustration. Each month they introduce a flower and then lead the reader through a series of simple line drawings that show how to portray it. At the start of the article there is a black-and-white photograph of the flower, and at the end of the article is the fully rendered illustration, which apparently any idiot housewife can duplicate.

This month the marsh gentian is the flower of choice. Instead of the usual single photograph of the flower at the beginning of the article, there are two. One photograph shows the flower open, and one shows it closed—the two states in which the walker is likely to discover it.

Enid likes the botanical illustration series. She likes reading about the flowers, and sometimes, on a rainy evening, she tries her hand at the illustration herself. It seems a useful thing to learn. Enid has a habit of judging the content of *Country Ways* in direct reference to her own preferences, and she would much rather learn to draw a flower than knit a pair of booties or frost a cake.

She starts reading about the marsh gentian. The flower is characterized by bright blue, trumpet-shaped blooms that are often striped with pale green. It has narrow leaves that grow in pairs up the stem of the plant. It blooms from July through October in acidic bogs and wet heathlands, can grow to a height of twelve inches, and is one of the few flowers that flourish in the transitional space between the mire of the bog and the firmer ground of the heath.

Enid goes back to Margaret's office, knocks delicately on the open door.

"Sorry," she says, "but that violet—the marsh gentian?—it's rare. There are only three places in England where it's ever seen. How is anyone supposed to draw it if they can't find it?"

Margaret takes off her glasses and pinches the bridge of her nose, which is red from where the Elastoplast has been rubbing against it. Enid tries not to stare but can't stop herself.

"That Saunders," Margaret says. "I should fire him. That's the second thing he's got wrong in this issue."

"He's just a writer," says Enid. "They make mistakes. Wasn't it proofed?"

"Yes, of course it was proofed."

Margaret sounds irritated, and Enid wants to point out that the fault lies not with her for bringing the error to Margaret's attention, but rather with the error itself. But she doesn't say this.

"Thank you, Enid," says Margaret. "I'll see to it."

Enid backs out of the office, but then comes in again. "What was the first thing?" she asks.

"What first thing?"

"The first thing Saunders got wrong."

Margaret sighs, puts her glasses back on again. "He misjudged the distance for 'A Ramble Round the Cotswolds.' Instead of a pleasant five-mile stroll, it's actually fifteen miles. If someone starts out for a nice walk after lunch, they'll be finishing it in darkness."

"Probably not finishing at all," suggests Enid. "More likely lost and stumbling around for ages. Perhaps never to be found again."

"Anything else?" Margaret sounds even more irritated.

"No." Enid leaves the office for the second time.

Back in her little corner of the art department, she looks at the two photographs of the marsh gentian. They might as well be completely different flowers. The closed flower, with its slender, tapering bloom, looks completely opposite to the open, star-shaped version of the violet. Even without the fact of it being a rare flower, the marsh gentian really was a ridiculous choice for illustration, because you would find the flower in one of those two states, either open or closed, but which one was really the true example of the specimen?

One of the three places in Britain where the flower is found is in the Ashdown Forest in East Sussex. Enid is reminded again of those days she spent exploring the forest almost ten years ago now. Wouldn't it be nice to go back there again and see the heath in all its glory?

But that thought is quickly followed by one of Rose. Enid doesn't know what has become of her. Perhaps she is still in Sycamore Cottage? Perhaps she has married and moved elsewhere? Enid has doubts about the likelihood of this second scenario. She doesn't remember seeing Rose with Toby, but she does remember seeing Rose happy, and she knows it was because of Toby. In the dimly lit vault of memory, she contrasts this happiness with what she remembers of Rose and James's wedding. She knows that Toby made Rose happier than James did, and that happiness would probably not be easy to set aside. So a jaunt down to see the Ashdown Forest in summer would inevitably lead Enid to Rose's cottage, and although she has, in many ways, remembered that time with Rose fondly, Enid is also fiercely loyal to her brother and won't do anything to upset him.

She looks again at the photographs of the marsh gentian. She will never see it in her lifetime. And just as twitchers make a list of birds they have spotted, Enid makes a list in her mind of some of the things she will never see again: a marsh gentian, the Ashdown Forest in summer, Rose.

WHEN ENID finally gets back to her flat, it's gone nine and she's exhausted. She kicks off her shoes and lies down fully clothed on the bed, trying to decide if she's more hungry or tired, if she should rouse herself to get something to eat or just go straight to sleep.

She decides on sleep, but then she hears a key turning in the lock, the sound of the flat door opening and closing, the tap of shoes as someone walks down the hallway towards the bedroom.

"Enid?" A head pokes around the door frame. "Fancy going to the Crown? It's half-price fish and chips night."

The Crown is as crowded as ever. Enid battles her way to the bar to get the drinks and place the order, then battles her way back again. By the time she returns to the table, she feels irritated and churlish.

"Someone trod on my foot," she says, slapping the drinks down on the wooden tabletop. "Right on the arch. Bloody painful. And he didn't even apologize. Bloody idiot."

"Darling." Margaret reaches over and squeezes Enid's hand. "Don't be cross. I've looked forward to seeing you all day."

"You have seen me all day." Enid leans down, slips her foot out of her shoe, and rubs it where it's been stepped on.

"Well, not how I like to see you," says Margaret.

"Oh, I don't know. I sometimes think you like to boss me around at the office more than you like being with me at home."

"That's not fair." Margaret takes a sip of her gin and tonic. "In fact, that's a horrible thing to say."

"Is it?" Enid slips her shoe back on. "Yes, I suppose it is. I'm sorry. I'm tired from all the travel, and from freezing to death all weekend in James's shepherd's hut."

"Well, you don't need to take it out on me."

"Who else am I meant to take it out on?"

Their supper arrives, and after the first few mouthfuls of fish and greasy batter, Enid feels more cheerful. "I did miss you," she says.

"You have a funny way of showing it."

"Come on, Mags. Can't we start again? I am sorry."

Margaret takes a healthy sip of her gin and tonic. "How was your brother?" she asks.

"Terrible. I don't think he eats, and he drinks too much. The cottage is so primitive he might as well be living in a cave. Probably warmer in a cave, come to think of it. He's so miserable that I don't think he can see how miserable he is." Enid puts down her knife and fork. "How would you feel about going down there for Christmas with me? We could give him a proper Christmas, cheer him up a bit."

"Have you told him about us, then?"

"No, not exactly." Enid takes a sip of her drink. "Not at all, really. But I'm going to write him and tell him this week." She takes another swallow of gin and tonic. "Or next week." She drains the last of her glass. "Definitely by Christmas."

"We could just go down as friends," says Margaret. "Workmates. Flatmates."

"Yes, that might be better."

"Colleagues," says Margaret. "That's the word for it."

"Well, it isn't at all the word for it," says Enid. "But it will have to do."

"It's not entirely a lie."

"No, not entirely." Enid crams the last of her chips onto her fork. "Will you come with me to Wales, then? To see James?"

"Yes, I will. I'd be happy to, in fact. It will be a nice change from sitting in my parents' stuffy parlour making small talk about my sister's brats and the allotment."

"Good." Enid pushes her plate away, feeling satisfied with both the conversation and her supper. "Shall I fetch us another drink?"

"That would be lovely."

But when Enid goes back to the bar, there on a stool at the end by the taps is George Fletcher from Sales.

"Where's my drink?" asks Margaret when Enid returns to the table empty-handed.

"Fletcher from Sales is sitting up at the bar."

"Do you think he saw you?"

"I don't think so. I kept my head turned."

Margaret grabs her purse from the bench beside her. "Shall I leave first, or will you?"

"I'll go. I'm already standing. Give me fifteen minutes' head start. I'll meet you by the tobacconist's near the park."

"Just meet me at home."

"Mags, couldn't we walk at least partway together?"

"I just can't risk it. You know how hard it's been for me. This could ruin everything."

"But we could just be having a drink together. An innocent drink."

"It's not innocent."

"But how is Fletcher to know that?"

"He would know." Margaret smooths her skirt. "He would see the way you look at me. The way I look at you."

There is to be no argument on the matter. Enid pushes her chair into the table. "I'll see you back at the flat, then."

Margaret is the only female editor at *Country Ways*, a fact that always strikes Enid as ridiculous, although she knows the struggle it's been for Margaret to achieve this level of success. Even Enid's own presence in the art department is out of the norm, and she has also had to fight hard for her lowly position of paste-up artist. And to think of all the jobs women used to do in the war, when the men were off fighting. There was nothing a woman couldn't do in those days, including flying commercial aircraft. Now the choice is between being a secretary or a nurse, or perhaps a teacher at a junior school. And these jobs are for the unmarried woman. The married woman's entire purpose in life is to be a loving wife and mother, serving her husband and children all day long, sitting down with a quick cup of tea in the afternoon to leaf through her latest copy of *Country Ways*.

Country Ways—read almost entirely by women and staffed almost entirely by men.

Enid lowers her head so she won't be recognized by Fletcher and walks quickly to the door of the pub, pushing it open and stepping outside into the cool night air.

Sometimes life seems very unfair. But right on top of thinking that, Enid thinks of all the men who died in the war, and how it made sense that those who didn't die—those who returned from fighting—would want their jobs back. It was their right, really, to try to pick up where they had left off, and they should be helped to do that, not blocked.

She lights a cigarette, thinks of Toby Halliday crashing his plane into the heath so close to Rose's cottage that it was hard not to believe he was heading straight for her. Enid half wishes she'd still been there, so Rose would have had her to lean on during the horror of that time, as she had had Rose to lean on, briefly, after Oliver's death. But that would have meant Rose's confessing about the affair with Halliday, and Enid wouldn't have wanted that secret, wouldn't have wanted to know anything that James didn't.

She starts walking along the pavement in the direction of the flat. Still. Rose had told her, eventually, although James knew too at that point. He'd had her letter asking for a divorce. Rose had then written Enid a short note after the plane crash. Enid can still remember most of it. She scuffs her foot through some fallen leaves. Her arch still hurts where that imbecile in the Crown stepped on it.

> *You might have heard about the plane crash on the forest. One of the airmen who died in that crash was the navigator, Toby Halliday. He was my lover, Enid. I mean, I loved him. And I don't know what to do now that he's gone. I don't know how to continue.*

That was basically it, Enid thinks, although she can't really be sure. It was so long ago now since she received that note, since she spent those weeks with Rose at Sycamore Cottage.

Enid had sent Rose a card with the words "I'm sorry" on it. She hadn't known what else to say because at that point she wasn't sure James knew anything about Toby Halliday. But now she wishes that she had said something else. Now that she's in love again herself—a complete surprise really, after all this time, and with someone she never expected to be in love with—Enid would tell Rose that she understands love is never the same. You can love different people over the course of a lifetime, but you won't love any two of them the same way, and quite frankly, you will love some of them more than others. A great deal more. If Toby was that to Rose—if he was the one she loved the most—then Enid would have said to her, "You will continue. But you will not recover. Don't expect that."

Enid was shocked to fall in love with a woman, but after getting over the initial astonishment, she realized that what had attracted her to Margaret was very similar to what had attracted her to Oliver. They were both rather imperious and, as they were used to being in charge at work, rather bossy. Enid, an elder child and a prefect at school, often found the role of being a leader burdensome, and so it was a relief to be bossed about by her lovers.

Another similarity was that there was no openness allowed in the relationships. Oliver had been married. Margaret was a woman, and she and Enid worked together. This similarity, Enid told herself, was an accident, but she sometimes wondered if it wasn't a little bit deliberate on her part, as if she couldn't entirely trust happiness, so she chose lovers with restrictive circumstances.

Rose never wrote to Enid again, and who can blame her. They had become close in that short time—another thing that had surprised Enid—and Rose must have expected more from her sister-in-law than a banal "I'm sorry."

Enid walks past Russell Square, her head full of Rose Hunter and the dark cottage on the edge of the forest where they spent six weeks together a decade ago. In another time, things might have turned out differently and they could have remained friends. Another time might be easier than this one, but there's only the time you're in, thinks Enid. And it's always going to be lacking somehow. Best to spend some of your moments here on earth noticing what else is here with you instead of concentrating solely on your own misery.

Thank god that James has his birds. The simple act of looking up must do something to make him feel better every day. It is a good thing, Enid thinks, to be curious about something outside of one's own thoughts and feelings. She and James are lucky because they are inclined this way, but Rose ... well, Enid is fairly sure that Rose is trapped largely inside herself and has no talent for observing the world around her.

A cat shoots by Enid in the darkness, startling her. There are so many more stray dogs and cats since the war, most having escaped from bombed-out buildings where their owners perished.

The war has been just as hard on animals as people, thinks Enid. She remembers the Regent's Park zoo broadcasting assurances at the start of the war that the public need not worry about dangerous animals escaping. The keepers had taken the precaution of killing all the poisonous snakes and insects. The polar bears and large cats had been locked inside tunnels to prevent their getting out in case a bomb hit the zoo.

One night the glass roof of the aviary was hit by a small bomb and three hummingbirds escaped, never to be found again. Enid smiles when she remembers the zoo's announcement that the public had nothing to fear from the hummingbirds, that they weren't considered dangerous. War made everyone so fearful. It was hard to believe that anyone could ever have thought to caution the public about a bird the size of a moth that drank the nectar of flowers.

~~~~~

BACK AT the flat, Enid undresses, puts on her nightie, brushes her teeth, and gets into bed. She knows that Margaret will wait a decent interval before following Enid out of the pub, and that decent interval could easily stretch to an hour. It will be so much better when Enid can leave *Country Ways* and work else-where, although the job prospects are rather dismal these days, and it could be months before she is able to find a suitable position.

The curtains haven't been pulled carefully and there is a gap between them of at least a foot. The streetlamps bleed into the room. Enid sits up against her pillows, switches off her bedside light. Through the gap in the curtains, she can see the dark lines of the trees in the park opposite. She feels she should get out of bed and close the curtains properly, but she's also lazy and warm now, so she does nothing, just lies there and frets a little, thinking of Rose again and how she used to walk the village streets of Forest Row looking for just this sort of crime.

It's not only love, thinks Enid. It's not only love that isn't the same again but every moment of a life. And just as one doesn't love two people the same way, one feels that some moments are much more important than others, but that often isn't apparent from the vantage point of the moment itself. From here—closing in on fifty, in a small flat in the middle of London, loving someone secretly, working at a job that some days has purpose and other days seems pointless—Enid can see which moments were the important ones in her life, and she is surprised to find that the time she spent with Rose in Sycamore Cottage is among them.

When she came to her sister-in-law, Enid was bombed out and in exile. And somehow from that place of exile, from the wandering she did up on the forest, and from her interaction with Rose and the dogs, she found herself on solid ground again. That cottage had felt, at first, like a prison, but in the end it had proved to be Enid's liberation.

She wishes she could thank Rose. Would it hurt, after all this time, to write her a letter? Would such a small act still count as a betrayal of James?

A key scrapes in the lock. The door to the flat creaks open. There's the knock as Margaret's shoes are kicked off and topple over on the tiles, then the pad of her stockinged feet down the long wooden hallway.

The bedroom door swings open and Margaret strides into the room. She takes a few confident steps and crashes into the end of the bed.

"It's pitch black in here," she says. "Are you trying to cripple me? Turn on a light."

She sounds irritable and tired, and she's being very selfish, thinks Enid. What if I had been asleep? This is what the years together bring, she thinks, switching on the bedside lamp—not distance brokered by reserve, but distance created by a sort of bullying familiarity. The voice one uses inside one's head, the private voice, eventually becomes the public voice, the voice that is used on one's lover.

Margaret rubs her knee, sits down on the end of the bed. Her hair has come loose from her scarf and twists in tendrils around her face. She must have hurried, thinks Enid, and her attitude towards Margaret softens in light of this new observation.

"Come to bed, Mags," she says. "It's late."

When Margaret is lying beside her in bed and the small lamp beside Enid has been switched off again, she realizes that she had meant to tell Margaret to pull the curtains, and because she forgot to do this, the gap in them is still there. The light from the streetlamp is still visible—as are the dark lines of the trees in the park opposite.

And suddenly Enid knows what happened to her during those weeks in Forest Row. She changed the way she saw the world. All those days of walking the heath, collecting her specimens, reinforced in her a need to look to the natural world for her own location. Now, even in London, she is constantly searching out the trees and grass, the flowers, to determine her position in the urban landscape. She looks to the natural world to guide her in how she moves through the city, in how she thinks about her own life.

Enid feels the clumsy fumbling beside her as Margaret searches for her hand under the bedclothes.

They lie on their backs in the London dark, holding hands, the light from the streetlamp ribboning in through the window. Enid wants to tell Margaret about Rose Hunter and the cottage in Forest Row, about what she has just decided about that time, but it's a long story now, and the hour is late. Margaret has to be in the office in the morning well before Enid.

"Remind me to tell you about Rose Hunter one day," she says.

"How will I possibly remember to do that?" says Margaret. She still sounds irritated, but anger is the place where Margaret's emotions land. It's where she goes when she feels tired, or ashamed, or frustrated, or sad. Sometimes it takes a very long time for Enid to parse out how Margaret is really feeling. She squeezes Margaret's hand, suddenly sorry for her.

"I wish we could have stayed in the pub," she says. "I was so looking forward to another drink with you, to a longer evening."

Margaret squeezes her hand back. "I know. Me too."

They turn at the same time so that they're facing each other, and they kiss.

"Better?" asks Margaret.

"Much."

It all seems right again. The worry about James drifts away. The annoyance at seeing Fletcher in the pub disappears, along with the busyness of the office that waits for them tomorrow and the problem of trying to keep their relationship secret. Now there are just the trees at the window and the warmth of their joined breath.

They kiss again, deeper and longer.

"What did you say about it in the end?" asks Enid, pulling away.

"Say about what?"

"The marsh gentian."

Margaret puts her hands under Enid's nightgown.

"I said that it is rare and one would be lucky to find it, but that the rarity makes it more desirable." Margaret struggles Enid's nightgown up and over her head. "I said that even though you might not find it if you look, you should look all the same—because if you do find it, there is nothing more beautiful."

"Oh, that's just right," says Enid. "Darling, that's just perfect."

Arctic Tern

Rose remembers how to negotiate the stairs so that they make no sound, stepping down them at the edges, avoiding the centre of the treads, where years of weight in the same place have worn the boards thin, causing them to groan and creak in protest when they are breached.

The front door is trickier. After the key has been turned in the latch, the heavy oak door must be opened by increments to stop it from squeaking. This takes ages, and Rose has to remind herself to be patient and not rush the job and ruin the chances of her escape.

Outside, the same care must be taken to close the door, but outside she can already feel her freedom and this task is not so freighted with worry. She eases the door closed, then presses her thumb down slowly on the latch to bring the massive door snugly back into place against the frame.

It's fifteen steps down the stone path to the gate. The gate also makes a noise when it is swung open, so Rose climbs it instead, dropping down soundlessly on the other side. Then there's just the road to cross and the ditch to navigate and she is up onto the forest.

This is when she misses the dogs the most, these first few steps onto the heath. She can almost see the blurred shapes of Harris and Clementine as they race away from her, ecstatic in the hull of morning, pounding their exuberant bodies to vapour.

But the dogs are dead. First Clementine, hit by a motor car one early morning four years ago, and then Harris, just last winter from cancer. Rose buried Harris on a small rise just outside Sycamore Cottage. Most mornings she goes and stands on the rise, watches the sun climb out of the hollows where it has slept all night. But this morning there isn't enough time to walk the distance across the top of the forest to the cottage where she used to live. This morning she goes instead to the patch of ground where the plane went down, where Toby Halliday was killed.

She had come up here as soon as she was allowed after the crash, when the site was no longer being guarded, when the bodies and the charred wreckage of the plane had been removed. She came to the place where Toby had died and she lay down in the crater caused by the crash, on the scorched earth, looking up at the sky and the tops of the distant birches. And even though the officials had scoured the ground for clues about the crash, digging down into the crater, Rose was still able to find a few items they had missed. She found the buckle end of a flight harness, most of it buried in the earth at the centre of the blackened grass. She found a brass button from an RAF flight jacket. And most disturbingly of all, she found a tooth, a front tooth, lying in a small depression by some stones.

Rose keeps the brass button around her neck on a chain, tucked down the front of her dress so that no one will see it. The oils and heat from her skin keep it shiny and polished. She keeps the burned buckle from the flight harness inside one of a pair of old shoes at the back of her wardrobe. The tooth she keeps wrapped in a handkerchief in the top drawer of her bureau.

There were six men who died in that plane crash, and Rose knows, logically, that probably none of the items belonged to Toby Halliday, and certainly not all three. But she has told herself over the years that the buckle, the button, and the tooth all came from him. Because aside from the rabbit's foot that the dogs took from his corpse, Rose has nothing left of her lover. Toby's possessions and his body were sent to the family. Rose had no legal right to anything of his, and so she is left with nothing.

The blackened grass has grown back green. The pit in the ground gouged out by the impact of the plane has filled in with bracken and wildflowers. None of the bodies of the airmen were buried at the site, but the village erected a marker to commemorate the crash. It resembles a tombstone and has the men's names etched on its grey granite face and the date they perished. It was placed at the edge of the crash site, and now that there is nothing left to distinguish the site, it looks orphaned, sitting in the middle of the tufted grass in the vast expanse of heath that is the Ashdown Forest.

Rose sits down with her back against the stone, draws her knees up to her chin. In the days after the accident, she would come up here and lie on the black grass and cry. When the monument was erected, she would sit as she is sitting now, with her back against the stone, sobbing. But it's been ten long years and all emotion has been spent. What she has now are the rituals associated with those old feelings, and there is still some comfort to be found from bending her body to those rituals.

It was decided that the crash was caused by engine failure and the subsequent loss of control of the aircraft. The last radio contact suggested that the plane was headed for the airfield at Penshurst to make an emergency landing, but the crew members clearly had to ditch it before they could reach there. None of the airmen were from the area, so Rose knows that it must have been Toby's idea to land on the forest. There is a measure of solace in this, in thinking that Toby tried to keep his promise and return to her.

The stone is hard against Rose's back. There is dew coating each blade of grass in front of her, misting the bases of the trees in the distance.

Already she has been away from the house longer than she meant to, but she feels too weary to stir herself. Again, she thinks of the dogs and longs for the way they leapt and bounded across the heath, recalls how movement for them was always joyful, full of purpose.

And just as Rose's body remembers her rituals of grieving, it remembers her attachment to the dogs, and she whistles for them without thinking, the sound dying away slowly, like the cry of a mournful, solitary bird.

BACK AT the house there is no creeping about to avoid detection. Constance is up and in full sail, sitting down to breakfast alone in the dining room.

"Where were you?" she asks as Rose tries to tiptoe past and escape back up the staircase.

"I went for a walk."

"There was no one here to boil my egg."

From the hallway outside the dining room, Rose can see that Constance has a boiled egg in front of her on her plate.

"I had to do it myself," says Constance, finishing Rose's thought.

"I'm sorry."

"Why do you need to go out for a walk anyway? You don't have that wretched dog anymore." Constance takes a slice of toast from the silver rack in front of her. "There's no reason for you to leave the house before I'm up."

"No. I suppose there isn't." Rose has given up arguing with her mother. She has found it easier just to agree with whatever Constance says. When she first moved in with her, after her father died suddenly of a heart attack, she had tried to defend herself from every accusation. But it was more wearing to argue back than it was simply to accept what was being said. And ultimately, all arguments reached the place where Rose couldn't argue back—the place where her mother reminded her that she had been taken in because she was a divorced woman and could no longer support herself. This was a place of shame for Rose, and she wanted to avoid going to it whenever possible.

"Is there anything you need me to fetch from the shops for you today?" she asks.

"Yes, as a matter of fact there is." Constance pushes aside her plate with the half-eaten egg and untouched piece of toast. An entire other adult could be fed with what Constance neglects to eat at each meal.

"What's that, then?"

"I need you to go into East Grinstead and buy me some new undergarments."

"Underpants?"

"Yes."

Oh, the unfairness of it all, thinks Rose, going into the dining room to clear her mother's plate—having to live in her parents' home again, as powerless and timid as the child she used to be.

It's EARLY closing, so East Grinstead is busier than usual when Rose steps off the bus into the high street. She delays purchasing the underpants, a small act of rebellion witnessed by no one and therefore pointless, and instead goes into the grocer to get some jam and chocolate biscuits for tea. The rationing has recently been lifted on chocolate biscuits, so Rose buys them every chance she gets. The war has been over for five years now, and yet there is still rationing for tea, sugar, meat, cheese, and sweets. Soap rations were recently lifted too, but it could still be years before all the rationing ends.

After rationing comes hoarding, and there are barely any packets of chocolate biscuits left in the shop. Rose has to make do with a single packet that she finds behind some tins, where it must have rolled in the grab and snatch of the mob that had emptied the biscuit aisle before she got there.

"Mrs. Hunter?" Rose looks up to see a man in a jumper and tweed jacket, his wavy brown hair escaping in tendrils from under a cap.

It has been so long since she was called by that name that it takes her a moment to realize the man is addressing her.

"Yes?"

"Gregory Spencer. You bought a dog once from my father. The sister of his dog, Clementine, I believe."

"Oh, yes." Rose doesn't remember Gregory.

"We never met," says Gregory, noticing her puzzled expression. "Not properly. I was away in Africa for the war, but I remember you from the village when we were children."

"How is your father?"

"Older. Less able. I'm back on the farm helping him these days." Gregory takes off his cap, runs a beefy hand through his hair. "He told me that your dog died?"

"Cancer," says Rose. "She died last Christmas. I still miss her so much."

"Well, Clementine's granddaughter has had a litter and there are some puppies left. You should come by and pick yourself one. There are some real beauties."

"I couldn't," says Rose, thinking of her mother's house and how any dog brought there would be left chained up in the garden for its whole miserable existence.

"Sorry to hear that." Gregory moves off a few paces, and then comes back. "Isn't it a sad thing," he says, "that in a full human life, we will have only five or six dogs? It doesn't seem enough, does it?"

"No, it doesn't."

"And that's if you have them one after the other." Gregory puts his hat back on, touches the brim with his finger. "If you change your mind, Mrs. Hunter, come and see us."

"I will. I mean, I won't. But thank you, Mr. Spencer."

"Gregory."

"Rose."

He walks away, and Rose has a moment of thinking how odd it was for them to use their first names at the end of their conversation rather than the beginning, as though they were just meeting.

Six pairs of high-waisted, extra-elasticized beige underpants later and Rose boards the bus just before the shops shut at lunch. She gets off in Forest Row, at the bottom of Ashdown Road, and walks up towards the edge of the forest.

Sycamore Cottage is closed up now. It hasn't been rented since Rose moved out. The windows are shuttered and the garden has grown wild. She tries the kitchen door, out of long-ago habit, but of course it is locked tight against intruders.

The mound where Harris is buried commands both a view of the forest and a view of the cottage. It has been dug recently enough that no grass has grown back on top of it. Rose stands on the small muddy hillock, looking first at Sycamore Cottage and then out over the expanse of heath at Broadstone Warren.

"It continues to be awful," she says to her dead dog in the ground beneath her feet. "More hellish every day. I wish you hadn't gone and left me to it."

Who would have thought that she would long for the war years, that they would be the height of happiness for her? It was ridiculous, really, when so many families wanted to forget the horror of that time. Yet here Rose was, trying to call it back every day, because it contained all the moments of pleasure that she would likely ever have.

OF COURSE she's late for tea, without even knowing what time it is when she returns. But if she hadn't been late for tea, then she would have trekked mud into the house, or forgotten to buy something at the shops, or worn the wrong colour skirt. Rose is convinced that her mother has a chart where she checks off her daughter's trespasses, of which there are an ever-increasing number daily.

"I nicked the last packet of biscuits," Rose says,

carrying a plate liberally covered with them into the sitting room, where her mother is ramrod straight in her wing chair by the fire, reading the newspaper.

"Chocolate biscuits," says Rose, and at that, Constance puts down her paper and takes one of the biscuits, nibbling round the edges like a mouse.

"You need a job," she says suddenly. "If you have no marriage prospects, then you should be put to work."

"There are no jobs for women these days," says Rose. "And I'm not really qualified for anything."

"Well"—Constance puts her half-eaten biscuit back on the plate with the uneaten ones—"you can't expect me to keep you forever. You'll have to think of something to do."

CONSTANCE KEEPS her bedroom door closed, and there is usually no reason for Rose to enter her mother's room. But today she goes in there to put away the underpants she purchased in East Grinstead. She carefully folds them into the top drawer of her mother's bureau and turns to leave, not wanting to linger in the room any longer than she has to. She sees it out of the corner of her eye, the photo on the table by her mother's bed. For all the years she can remember, there has always been a photograph there of her father as a young man, leaning on a stile near a wood, hatless, sleeves rolled up, the knot of his tie loose. In that photograph his head is thrown slightly back, as though the picture was taken while he was laughing.

That photograph is gone. In its place—in the same frame, even—is a picture of a young man in a hat and greatcoat. William, Constance's first husband, dressed for the first war, just married and looking like a child.

THAT NIGHT, Rose sits on the edge of her bed, fully dressed. She doesn't have a light on and her curtains are pulled expertly across the windows, so there's no leakage from outside.

Nights are the worst. In the daytime, Rose can busy herself with all the trivial tasks of existence, but at night there is less to do and she is left alone with her thoughts, none of which offer her any mercy.

Who knows what she feels anymore? It's all so long ago, and yet she's held there, unmoving, playing everything over and over in her mind.

James did love her after all. She should have waited for him, should never have written to him asking for a divorce. They could be living happily together right now. James's book was a success. He would find it easy to get a position, and often there was a house that went with an observatory. Rose and the children would make that house their own.

Or, Toby didn't die in the aeroplane crash, didn't even crash, but survived the war and came back to Rose, as they had hoped he would. They would marry after Rose's divorce came through and travel together, living a life of adventure and pleasure, moving from one exciting place to another.

The emotions are gone. Rose is left with the facts, the husk of her life's experience, not the kernel of feeling that exists at the centre of it all.

The truth is that you do forget people. When you conjure them up, long after they have gone, you can't recall the essence of them, just the outline.

Rose loved James and betrayed him. Or, Rose never loved James and finally found the right man in

Toby, only to have him die. Either way, it ends badly for Rose. In the first story she is guilty. In the second she is heartbroken.

Rose extracts the brass uniform button from between her breasts. It is warm from lying against her skin. She holds it to her lips, lets it fall back down the front of her dress.

She moves through the familiar dark of the bedroom—this room that was hers as a child and still has the same sparse furniture—and slides open the top drawer of her bureau. She carefully unwraps the handkerchief that holds the tooth, and then, just as carefully, slips the tooth into her mouth, feeling the cold clink of it against her own teeth, the smooth square of enamel lozenge lying on her tongue, the small weight of it like a word just before it's said.

ROSE REMEMBERS the way, even though it's been years since she was last there. She leaves her mother's house the next morning on the pretext of going to the village, but she walks instead across the heath, then along the road and up the muddy farm lane.

There's no answer at the front door. She walks round the side of the house, towards the barn, and finds Gregory out near the chicken coop.

"Hello there." He looks up from his task of spreading feed over the ground in front of the enclosure. "Changed your mind, then?"

"Yes. No. I can't have one, but I thought I'd come and take a look at them anyway." Rose leans on the fence, watching the chickens peck at the feed. "I used to have chickens. During the war."

"Stupid creatures really." Gregory shakes out the last of the tin pail, opens the gate, and comes over to where Rose is standing.

"I didn't mind them," says Rose. "Their needs were simple, easy to meet."

Gregory puts the metal pail on the ground, wipes his hands on his coveralls. "Come on, then," he says. "Let's take you to see those pups."

The dogs are in a horse stall in the barn. Four white puppies with brindle markings. They are curled up with their mother in the straw when Rose and Gregory first get to them, but they immediately wake up when they hear the human voices.

Gregory opens the half door on the stall, and he

and Rose step inside. The puppies try to climb up their legs. Rose kneels down and lets them clamber over her. Their joyful energy makes her feel like crying.

"They're all bitches," says Gregory, bending down to pick one up and let it lick his face. "There were seven pups altogether. The others have gone."

"They're adorable."

"I'm going to keep one for myself, but the rest need to find homes. Soon. They're getting too old to leave contained, and they wreak havoc in the barn if I let them out. Yesterday they knocked over the milking pail and drank all the milk." Gregory hands the puppy he's been holding to Rose. "Wouldn't you reconsider, Mrs. Hunter?"

"I can't," says Rose, but she tucks the puppy under her chin, inhaling the sweet puppy smell on the top of its head. "And I'm not Mrs. Hunter anymore."

"Oh, I'm terribly sorry. I didn't realize."

"No, no. James didn't die," says Rose. "I divorced him. He was a prisoner in Germany for the entire war, and I didn't wait for him to return. Now I live with my mother because I can't afford to be on my own. She despises dogs and won't allow them in the house. Poor Harris had to spend her last years out of doors. I couldn't do that to another dog." She hands the puppy back to Gregory. "I'm sorry." She feels a little emotional at having said so much, blames it on the wriggling high spirits of the puppies shaking something loose in her.

Gregory places the puppy gently on the floor of the horse stall. He straightens up, touches Rose lightly on the shoulder. "Come in and say hello to Dad," he says. "He would like the chance to see you while you're here."

ROSE WALKS back across the forest. It's a dull day, the clouds low and threatening, wind bending the grasses. She bought some eggs from the Spencers, but it is not the same as having been to the shops in the village, and she will no doubt be caught out in her lie. It is so strange to be thrust backwards in her life, back to when she was a child, trying to hide what she was doing from her mother's critical bullying.

There's a movement up ahead in the bracken. A fox, standing still and sniffing the air in the direction of Rose's approach. She stops and they regard each other.

And then, out of the sky a bird appears, shrieking above her head. Rose is used to gulls, blown inland from the sea and wheeling across the heath. But there is something in the shape of this bird that is wrong. Its body is slender as a dart. Its beak is bright orange. And its behaviour is not exactly gull-like. True, it is as angry as any gull, but usually a gull's anger is not attached to anyone, but rather is just a general complaint—at finding itself too far inland, at realizing it has to fight the wind to get back to the shore and any hope of food. Gulls are irritable, squawking to voice that irritation to everything around them.

But this bird is directly upset with Rose. It dives towards her, stalls just feet from her head, back-paddling up into the sky, wings and tail spread, screaming. At first Rose thinks the fox has disturbed it, but the bird takes no notice of the fox. All its attention is focused on Rose. She wonders if she has wandered near its nest, but gulls are shorebirds. They won't have a nest out in the middle of an open field. They make their nests on the ledges of cliffs or on rocky islands offshore, where they will be free from predators. She knows this much from having been briefly married to someone who liked to study birds.

The bird dives at Rose once more, pulls back just in the nick of time, dives at her again. She covers her head with her arms, dropping the box of eggs in the process. The fox, unconcerned with the attack by the bird, sits on its haunches twenty yards ahead, waiting for Rose to move off so it can have at the broken eggs.

The bird is so angry, but Rose can't think what she has done to merit this anger. She stumbles across the field with the bird diving repeatedly at her head, only circling up and away once she reaches the road.

Back at the house she looks it up in the bird guide, a present to her father from James. It seems to be an Arctic tern—a bird that migrates between the Arctic and Antarctic, a distance travelled of over twenty thousand miles each year. It has the farthest migration of any bird; the Arctic tern essentially lives in the air.

Suddenly the behaviour of the bird makes sense to Rose. It might have no real experience of people, flying between such remote locations that when it does touch down, it does so in empty landscapes. It could be that she was the first human the bird had ever seen, and while it could recognize the fox as being from its world, clearly Rose was not seen as a creature of the earth. There is nothing natural about a human being, thinks Rose, even though we pretend, all the time, that this isn't the case at all.

THERE ARE a lot of rules for Rose, living in her mother's house. She is sure there are more restrictions than the first time she lived here, but she has no choice except to obey.

Bathing is allowed only once a week, and only at night, never in the afternoon. All lights must be out by ten o'clock. If Rose is reading and a light shows under her door, her mother will rap on the door from the hallway until the light is switched off. No music from the wireless, and no singing. Listening to the evening news is permitted, but the wireless is turned off after the broadcast is over. No mud in the house. No eating between meals. No tears.

The list goes on and on. Rose can't even remember all the rules, but she's learned to fit herself into the spaces around them. At night, if she can't sleep, she opens her window wide and sits on the sill, her legs dangling down over the bricks. She likes the feel of the night air on her skin, the soft sound of the owls in the pines at the back of the garden. For her weekly bath, she fills the tub right up to the brim and stays in it for as long as possible. She never sings in the house, but she sings outside, at full volume, when she is crossing the heath. She cries all the time.

Tonight Rose begs off listening to the news with her mother, saying that she has to write a letter to an old friend, and she goes to her bedroom and closes the door.

There is no letter. There are no friends. Rose lost touch with most of her schoolmates when she married James. And afterwards ... well, even though she and Toby were careful, it seems the story of their affair had leaked out somehow, and by the time Rose divorced, the sentiment against her was such that it would have been hard to make a friend of anyone in the village.

Mostly she doesn't care. Mostly she would just prefer to have Harris back, to have dog company over human company.

But tonight, sitting in her room, watching the sky darken slowly outside her window, she thinks of Gregory Spencer, of his kindness at not commenting on her confession, of his easy manner, and she wishes she could go to see him again. But there is no reason to go back to the farm. She can't have a dog, and it would be painful to see the puppies again and know that she couldn't tuck one under her arm and bring it home with her.

Rose goes over to the window and opens it, leans her body across the sill, looking down into the back garden. She used to do this as a child, calling out to her father while he raked the leaves or dug the beds. He would always stop what he was doing and wave to her, sometimes doffing his cap in her direction.

She misses her father, misses the alliance she shared with him against Constance, but she also doesn't blame him for dying, and she always knew he would go first. His bluff and banter was no match for the steely freight of his wife. The strong don't necessarily survive, but the mean invariably do.

He would have been interested in the Arctic tern over the heath today. He would have laughed at the outrage of the bird on encountering a person for the first time. Frederick, like his daughter, made no secret of preferring the natural world to the human one.

There was a lot of her father in Toby, thinks Rose. They were similarly easygoing. And now they are similarly dead. She hauls her body back over the sill and closes the window.

HE COMES to the front door in the morning, after breakfast, when Constance is upstairs dressing for her biweekly bridge game with the retired colonel, his wife, and her widowed sister. Rose is in the kitchen doing the washing-up. The window above the sink faces out onto the front garden, so she sees him coming up the path and intercepts him before he has a chance to knock on the door and alert Constance.

Rose steers Gregory back down the path, through the gate, and out onto the road in front of the house.

"Sorry," she says, "but my mother will come down if she sees you."

"And that would be bad?"

"Terrible." Rose manoeuvres Gregory behind

the big yew hedge that borders the garden, where she knows they can't be spotted from the house. "My mother is not like your father. She's not a nice person."

Yesterday, old Mr. Spencer had made Rose switch chairs with him in the parlour so that she could enjoy the view out the window over the fields while she sipped her tea.

Gregory takes off his cap. Rose can see that his hands have been scrubbed clean. The dirt that was under his nails yesterday is gone.

"I came to say two things to you," he says, looking her square in the eyes. "The first is that I was engaged to be married when I left to fight overseas, but my girl didn't wait for me to come back. She left me while I was away, sent a letter to me in Africa to say that she was breaking off the engagement."

Rose feels her heart sink. "I'm sorry," she says.

"No. Don't be. I was gone five years. That's too long a time to wait for someone. To remain faithful to me, she would have had to stop living her life." Gregory worries the brim of his hat between his fingers. "Why, if I loved her, would I want her to do that for me?"

"But weren't you heartbroken?"

"For a time. Yes. But I understood and so I forgave her. I didn't hold it against her."

Rose can feel the tears start in her eyes, tries to blink them away. "What's the second thing?" she asks.

Gregory Spencer smiles. He has crooked front teeth and lots of lines around his eyes that suggest he's used to smiling.

"I wanted to say that if you've had a dog, then you should have another. If you've had a dog, then it's hard to do without one."

"But I can't have a dog. I've already said that."

"You can't have a dog here. You could, however, keep the dog at my farm and come and see it whenever you want, until your situation changes and you are able to have it with you all the time."

"But I don't see my situation ever changing."

"All situations change," Gregory says. "We've both learned that, haven't we?"

Rose lets the tears roll down her cheeks, doesn't try to wipe them away. She doesn't know what upsets her more, the kindness she's being shown or the lack of it she's lived with for so long. She leans in towards

Gregory Spencer, buries her face in the shoulder of his coat. He puts his arms around her and gives her a squeeze.

"Come now," he says. "No need for tears. It's a happy occasion, not a sad one. Fetch your coat and let's go and pick you out a new dog."

Cedar Waxwing

CHRISTOPH WALKS ACROSS THE QUADRANGLE TO his office. His boot heels ring on the stones, the strike of each foot echoing through the courtyard.

There are three flights of stairs to climb, with a rest on each landing before continuing. At each rest he leans against the banister, looking out the small stairway window, measuring his progress by the diminishing square of stone and trees below.

It's been almost a week since he was in his office, and there is a stack of mail for him in the mailbox near the department secretary's desk. He takes the letters and packages, not bothering to look at them, and drops them on the edge of his desk when he gets inside his office.

Christoph removes his coat and hangs it on the rack by the door, tucks his briefcase beside the desk on the floor. He opens the shutters on the window. He sits down.

Most of the letters are unremarkable—colleagues asking for favours, publishers trying to entice him to buy a particular book—but there is one small package whose postmark is unfamiliar. He turns it over in his hands, examining the cramped script on the brown paper, the foreign stamp. Finally he slits the sealed flap with his letter opener, extracts a folded piece of paper, and reads the single page.

Dear Kommandant,

It seems strange to address you using that term, but since that is the only way I knew you, I would find another form of address even more difficult.

I pray that this letter finds you. I remember that you worked at the university in Berlin and so have sent this parcel there, hoping that, if you survived the war, you will have resumed your duties in the classics department.

I am writing to you because for years I have

thought of that day when you took me from the camp with a mixture of confusion and terror. You may remember that I believed you were removing me from the camp to be shot. But this morning, on what will be my last morning, I suddenly saw it all differently because I am no longer afraid, and I wanted to finally thank you for taking me to see the cedar waxwings. I can understand now what an extraordinary act of kindness it was, and I am grateful. Kindness should never go unacknowledged. I am enclosing the book I wrote on the redstarts that were around our camp. I hope you will see, when reading it, that I did indeed make a proper study of the birds.

The waxwings were beautiful, were they not? Chatting and busy in the tops of the pine trees. Such sleek little fellows. Such a soft, pale yellow. I wish we could go to visit them together again now that the war is well over.

Flight is not the astonishing thing. I have always thought that the miracle of birds is not that they fly, but that they touch down.

Yours truly,

James Hunter

Christoph folds the letter, puts it down on top of his desk, and slides the book from the package. It is a slim volume with a coloured illustration of a redstart on the front and the single word "Redstart" above the bird with James Hunter's name below.

Christoph's hands are shaking. What a strange thing it is to receive this book and letter, for the past to rise up and meet him here.

He remembers very clearly the day he took James Hunter to see the waxwings.

It had been unusually cold the night before. His body was stiff from the cold when he awoke. He remembers shaving in the early morning before setting out on his journey to visit a friend who was in command of a smaller prison camp sixty miles distant from his own. He remembers dragging the razor slowly across the stubble on his cheeks, making faces in the mirror to flatten out the planes of his face and avoid any nicks from the blade.

The mirror was small, which meant that Christoph had to stand a certain distance from it in order to view the whole of his face. This distance was farther than he could see without his glasses, so he wore them for the shave but had to constantly remove them to wipe the steam from the lenses.

Aging is an annoyance, he had thought at the time. And right after that, War is a young man's game.

It seemed unfair to be made to participate in another war at the age of forty-six, an age when he should have been feeling the waning of ambition and enjoying his position at the university. But many soldiers who had distinguished themselves in the first war were appointed to command positions in prisoner-of-war camps. His predicament was not unusual.

Christoph had driven himself that morning because he liked to have time alone, and there was precious little of that at the camp. He also wanted to feel, just for one day, not like a man in control of two thousand English officers, but like the classics professor he had once been. He wanted to imagine he was living that relatively uncomplicated life again, merely going for a drive, merely visiting a friend.

The drive out in the morning was slow and peaceful. He arrived at Wilhelm's camp in time for lunch. They ate and drank well. He had felt relaxed in his friend's company—more relaxed than he'd been for months. It was a relief to be out of the camp, not to feel the burden of his command pressing down on him every minute of every day as he waited for the war to end and his life to resume its familiar shape.

Perhaps it was the wine, or perhaps it was the loosening of the clamp he always kept tightened down on his emotions, but halfway through the drive back to his camp, Christoph started to panic. He hadn't wanted the war, hadn't welcomed it, was surprised to have been given a command. He wasn't a member of the Nazi Party and was, frankly, afraid of their swagger and cruelty. When SS officers came to perform inspections of his camp, Christoph was always nervous and tried to move them through quickly. He didn't want them to linger and find any discrepancies with how he ran things. When prisoners escaped, he tried to make sure they were brought back alive. He believed in the Geneva Conventions and upheld their principles. But even so, the war was working its way into his bones.

The day before, he had been sitting at his desk in his office and had heard what he thought was birdsong. He'd stood up and made his way to the window, just in time to see one of the guards shoot a prisoner through the head while he tended his little garden in front of the bunkhouse. The casualness of the act had shocked Christoph so deeply that he forgot to breathe for a minute or two. The prisoner's beautiful song had drawn the Kommandant to the window, the same song that had infuriated the guard and driven him to murder. It was yet another example of the difference that existed between Christoph and the men around him.

He wanted to be out of the war. He missed his wife so acutely that he either was overwhelmed by memories of her or couldn't recall her face. The pain of missing her brought her back in full force or not at all, as though his mind couldn't decide which would be the easier state for him to bear, and so offered him both at once.

His friend at lunch was full of bravado, seemed to prefer his new life as Kommandant to his old life as a civil engineer. Christoph did not want that to happen to him. He was finding it hard to get the execution of the gardening prisoner out of his head.

He pulled the car off the rutted road, stopped the engine, and walked out into the darkening landscape. It was early evening. He trudged over the stiff grass towards a copse of trees at the edge of the road.

He walked into the trees, hoping to clear his head of the clamour of his anxious thoughts.

At first Christoph thought the murmuring of the birds was the wind in the top branches of the trees, but it became louder, more distinct, and when he stopped to listen, when he looked up, he saw the bobbing heads of the cedar waxwings, their slick plumage pale against the dark green of the pines.

Christoph has always liked birds. When he was a boy he had collected eggs and nests. He would go out in the early mornings to look for different varieties to add to his species list.

He knew that the cedar waxwing, while native to North America, was rarely seen in Europe. He had seen Bohemian waxwings only once before, when he was that boy who rose early and went out into the world with a notebook and a pair of spyglasses.

Christoph looked at the birds in the trees. He thought of the prisoner in his camp, Hunter, who had been watching the redstarts down by the river. Hunter had probably never seen a waxwing. The birds were as rare in Britain as they were in Germany. Perhaps Christoph would bring the prisoner here tomorrow to see the cedar waxwings. He would show Hunter that they were not so different as men. The war may have separated them, but their love of nature joined them together. It would be a small but humane gesture, to take a prisoner out of camp for the day, to bring him here to see the birds.

The thought pleased him and he walked out of the trees, got into his sedan, and drove back to camp.

CHRISTOPH LOOKS down at the letter on his desk. Another death to add to the countless others that occurred in his POW camp. He rests his head in his hands, feels emotion rise like bile in his throat. He wishes that he could write to his former prisoner and tell him to wait out the awful, urgent moment he is in; tell him that the moment, like all moments, passes, and the feelings with it. But it's too late for that. Hunter's last morning must be almost a week old now. Any letter Christoph writes and sends would be useless, would never reach the living James Hunter.

But he is touched that James would reach out to him, that after all this time, through the war and its aftermath, James Hunter would remember so vividly that day when Christoph took him to see the waxwings. It's a day that Christoph remembers with equal clarity. It was a moment that felt blessed, in the midst of thousands of other moments that were not the least bit redemptive. Christoph is not proud of many things that happened in the war, but perhaps he is a little proud of that moment in the pines with James Hunter and the cedar waxwings.

He turns the book over in his hands and opens it, looking for a photograph of the author, but there is none. Just a note on the endpapers that says, "James Hunter works at a bird observatory in Wales and is writing a book about seabirds."

What an achievement, to turn those days of imprisonment into study, and that study into a book. Christoph may not be able to do anything to help his former prisoner, but he will remember him, and he will sit here this afternoon and read James Hunter's book on the redstart from beginning to end.

He stands up, goes over to the window, and looks down into the courtyard below. Students cross the square, hurrying to their lectures. One girl's red scarf blows off and she bends to pick it up. A man with dark hair pauses by a tree to light a cigarette.

From above, the people are only patches of colour, streaks of movement, the noise of their shoes on the quadrangle stones, the arc of their shadows leaning away from their bodies.

Mallard

JAMES DECIDES TO WALK TO THE POSTBOX TO MAIL
the letter, rather than leave it on his kitchen table to
be found afterwards. He doesn't trust that whoever
discovers his body will choose to post the letter. The
German name and address on the envelope might
put them off. There is still a lot of anti-German
sentiment about.

James wears his suit. It seems appropriate to
dress up. He would wear his suit if he were going on a
journey, or to meet his sister at the bus. Killing one-
self seems oddly, and similarly, formal. An event.

He walks quickly over the fields. The postbox is
by the bus stop. He wants to get there swiftly, post
the letter, and hurry back while it is still morning.

James does all the business of a day in the morning, and today, even given the macabre nature of the task, there will be no exception. Start early, he has always said to himself. Start early if you mean to get anything done.

There is only one letter to post, and it's tucked carefully away in the inside pocket of his suit jacket. James hasn't written to his sister, even though he has thought about it. But he doesn't know what to say beyond "I'm sorry," and he just can't bring himself to post a letter that contains only those two words. Instead, he has left a note on top of the notebooks where he has written his findings on the seabirds he's been studying. He has put the notebooks on his kitchen table, and the note simply says, "For Enid." His sister will know what to do with the notebooks, will decide if there is enough information in them to publish or if she will merely keep them to read through occasionally, as a sort of memorial to her brother.

It's a cool morning, sunny. The grasses in the field ripple in the wind and James brushes his hand along the tops of them as he walks to the village. He likes the soft, feathery feel of them under his hand.

It is a simple thing to post the letter, to drop it through the mouth of the letterbox. The walk out was all about this task. The walk back is all about what James will do when he returns to the cottage. This will be the last time he makes the journey from the village across these fields. What he thinks, on the return, is that he won't even stop at the cottage. Everything is in order there. He will just keep walking, past the cottage, straight off the edge of the cliff. That seems the easiest thing to do. There's an efficiency to it that pleases him.

It is a cowardly act, and James feels that he is a coward to do it. All through the war he kept himself alive, kept himself safe, only to give it all up now in the peace. But he is tired of the nightmares, the emptiness in his chest; he is tired of drinking to feel better, and then not feeling better at all. He simply wants it all to stop. He simply wants to fly off the top of the cliff and be done with it.

But this is not what happens.

James nears the end of the field and startles a flock of ducks that are floating in a large puddle in a flooded ditch by the track. They beat up into the air, the chatter of their wings as they flap together mimicking the exact sound of the cry of a single duck. The creaking of the wings as they move into flight sounding as a lone squawk.

James stops, his head back, watching the ducks as they climb into the sky, the sound of their wings fading slowly. How odd, he thinks, that the collective is the echo of the individual. And then he thinks, How wonderful. What a perfect machine the ducks are. How beautiful that one mallard's voice is carried aloft by the flight of his companions.

And suddenly he can see how he belongs to all of it—to the morning and the ducks, to the men who were in the cage with him during the war, to his sister, even to Rose when she was his bride and their life together was new and untried. He has a place in every one of them. He is carried forward by their lives, even though those lives are largely lived without him now.

The redstarts too—that pair on the stone wall that he watched so fiercely through the war—those birds and their descendants lift his captive soul up with them every time their little feathered bodies rise into the air. The line of their flight reaches all the way back to him here.

James hurries along the track, trying to get home as soon as possible. He has already missed hours of work today. He doesn't want to miss any more.

The morning breaks open, new and beautiful before him.

Author's Note

WHILE A WORK OF FICTION, THIS NOVEL IS BASED on three actual events.

There was a Wellington bomber that crashed on the Ashdown Forest during the Second World War, killing all members of the six-man crew.

There was a German prison camp Kommandant who took a prisoner to see some cedar waxwings in a nearby forest.

And there were birdwatchers during the war in some of the prison camps. One of these wartime birdwatchers, John Buxton, wrote a book about the redstart that is still regarded by many as one of the most comprehensive single-species studies ever undertaken.

Acknowledgments

I WOULD LIKE TO THANK MY AGENT, CLARE Alexander, for her belief in this book, and for her wisdom about how to improve it.

My Canadian editor, Jane Warren, and my US editor, Jenna Johnson, offered precise and invaluable editorial suggestions. Thank you for making this story better.

I would also like to thank managing editor Noelle Zitzer. It is always such a pleasure to work with you.

Heartfelt thanks as well to my UK editor, Rebecca Gray, and my Italian editor, Andrea Bergamini.

The Canada Council for the Arts, the Woodcock Foundation, and the Access Copyright Foundation all provided financial assistance during the writing of this book, for which I am very grateful.

Thanks to Glenn Hunter for the title.

My family and friends make my writing life possible, but I would particularly like to thank Nancy Jo Cullen for her love and support during the writing of this novel.